The

The Fifth Classic Diner Mystery

From *New York Times* Bestselling Author

Jessica Beck

A BAD EGG

Other Books by Jessica Beck

The Donut Shop Mysteries

Glazed Murder
Fatally Frosted
Sinister Sprinkles
Evil Éclairs
Tragic Toppings
Killer Crullers
Drop Dead Chocolate
Powdered Peril
Illegally Iced
Coming July 2013: Deadly Donuts

The Classic Diner Mysteries

A Chili Death
A Deadly Beef
A Killer Cake
A Baked Ham
A Bad Egg

The Ghost Cat Cozy Mysteries

Ghost Cat: Midnight Paws

Jessica Beck is the *New York Times* Bestselling
Author of the Donut Shop Mysteries from
St. Martin's Press
and
Author of The Classic Diner Mystery Series
and The Ghost Cat Cozy Mysteries
from Cozy Publishing

To my mother, Ruby;
a real jewel!

A Bad Egg by Jessica Beck; Copyright © 2013

All rights reserved.

Chapter 1

When Gordon Murphy originally left town, everyone said good riddance, especially Ellen Hightower, our morning waitress at The Charming Moose, a quaint little diner my family and I run in Jasper Fork, North Carolina. My grandfather, our diner's namesake Moose, had always called Gordon a bad egg, and no one but Ellen had ever had much cause to disagree with him. Like many girls who were not quite women yet, Ellen had gone out with Gordon initially *because* he was a bad boy, not in spite of it. She'd believed in her heart that she could change him, if only she had the chance, but five years into a hasty marriage, and two kids later, Gordon hadn't changed one bit, and, to no one's surprise, he left them in the middle of a snowy night in December. As far as anyone knew, Gordon never gave another thought to his ex-wife and his children after he filed for divorce a year later, but that all changed the day he came back to town five years after he'd first left. Just as summer follows spring, I suppose that it was inevitable that mayhem would ensue, and as things always seemed to go, they centered around me and my extended family at The Charming Moose.

"Gordon, I told you last night. You can't have my children." The second I heard Ellen's voice, I knew that there was trouble.

I hadn't been up front when Gordon Murphy slipped into the diner, or I would have told him that he wasn't welcome at The Charming Moose. I'd been in back chatting with my mother, who ran the grill from six to eleven in the morning.

"They're my kids, too," Gordon answered calmly as I walked out front.

"You gave them up the day you walked out on us," Ellen said. She was physically shaking, and her voice quivered a bit, but she wasn't about to back down. Normally, Ellen was a woman who was content with her life, and I knew that our customers appreciated her soft smile and the kind words she dished out along with the food she served.

This woman was someone different altogether, a mother bear fighting for her cubs, and if I were Gordon, I'd watch my next words very carefully. There were a handful of folks eating at the diner, but no one was about to make a sound for fear of upsetting the scene.

"That's not how the law sees it," Gordon said almost cordially. "I've consulted with my attorneys, and they believe that I have a solid case for joint custody."

"You're bluffing. *You* couldn't afford to hire anyone."

Gordon shrugged. "I've changed, Ellen. I'm doing fine now on my own, and with Jessie's support, the kids will have a better life once we're married than they've ever had with you."

"You told me last night how rich she was, but that doesn't mean a thing." Her voice faltered a little as she said it.

"Ellen, let's be reasonable," Gordon said.

I planned to stay out of it, since Ellen was doing just fine on her own, but when I saw her reach down to the counter to grab the sharp serrated knife that Malcolm Mason had recently used for his steak and eggs, it was time to move in.

I grabbed the knife before she could, and for one split second, Ellen looked at me with a feral expression. It was gone nearly as fast as it had appeared, but it scared me nonetheless.

It was time to put a stop to this. "Gordon, you need to leave the diner, and I mean right now."

"I don't see why I should. I have as much right to be here as anyone else," he said.

"Funny, that sign says that you don't," I answered as I pointed to the printed sign under the register. I could kiss my grandfather for installing it when he'd first opened the diner.

It allowed us the right to refuse service to anyone we pleased, and I'd used it myself on more than one occasion in the past.

"I'm not asking for service. I just want to talk to my wife."

"Ex-wife," Ellen said, spitting out the words. "And as far as I'm concerned, there's nothing left to talk about."

"That's where you're mistaken," Gordon said, and I knew that he'd pushed her too far with his last comment.

"Know one thing, Gordon," she said icily. "I'll see you dead before you get my children."

Gordon looked pleased by the threat as he looked around the dining room. "You all heard her just threaten me, didn't you?"

I smiled brightly at him. "I'm sorry. Did you say something? I was lost in my thoughts. I missed all of your conversation."

A frown appeared on Gordon's face as he looked around the room and realized that no one was looking at him now. "So that's the way you're going to act? Mark my words. You'll all pay for this."

I was about to say something when Ellen's dad, Robert Hightower, came storming into the diner. He was the very definition of an overprotective father, and when it came to his grandchildren, there was nothing that could keep him from defending them.

"Get out, you worthless piece of garbage," Robert said. He normally had a bit of a stammer when he spoke, but there wasn't a hint of hesitation in his voice right now.

"I'm warning you, old man. If you try something with me, I'll beat you just like I beat your little girl's boyfriend last night."

That was news to me. What had gone on the night before at Ellen's place? She had come into work that morning a little quieter and more subdued than normal, but she hadn't said anything about an earlier confrontation with her ex-husband. And who was this boyfriend? Was Ellen keeping secrets from me?

"You sucker-punched Wayne, and you know it," Ellen

said, and at least that part became clear. She and the mechanic had been flirting for months, but I hadn't realized that it had progressed beyond that. "He'd kill you in a fair fight."

"Let him know that I'm ready any time," Gordon said.

"There won't be enough left of you after I'm through," Robert said as he started toward Gordon. The younger man had thirty years on his former father-in-law, but I wouldn't have placed any bets on a confrontation between them at the moment. Robert was vigorous and swarthy, and I didn't doubt that he could do some real damage to his opponent, given the level of his motivation.

"Hang on here, folks," Sheriff Croft said as he walked into the diner. "Everybody just take a deep breath."

"Sheriff, I asked Gordon to leave, and he refused. I'd appreciate it if you'd escort him out," I said.

"Is that true?" the sheriff asked as he looked at Gordon.

"Listen, I know that none of you like me, but that doesn't mean I don't have rights."

"You do for a fact," the sheriff said, "but the lady asked you politely to leave her diner, which is well within *her* rights, and if you continue to refuse, I'm going to show you the inside of my jail, not that you haven't already seen it more than once in the past."

"Fine, I'll go for now, but this isn't over," Gordon said as he stared at Ellen.

"I meant what I said," she answered.

The sheriff started to walk behind Gordon as he headed for the door, and Robert Hightower followed close behind.

"Where do you think you're going?" the sheriff turned and asked him.

"I thought I'd stretch my legs a little," Robert said as he looked intently at Gordon.

"Why don't you let me buy you a cup of coffee in a second, and we can talk," the sheriff said, and then he turned to me. "Victoria, set him up, would you?"

"Thanks, but no thanks," Robert said.

The sheriff shook his head, and then he took a step closer to Ellen's father. "It wasn't exactly a request, Bob." I'd never heard anyone but Robert Hightower's closest friends call him Bob. It seemed to do the trick.

"You're not worth it, anyway," he said to Gordon with a sigh.

Ellen's ex just smiled, and I thought Robert might come after him because of the grin alone, but he calmed down, and I said, "Let's get you that coffee."

He nodded, and Ellen took her father's arm and guided him to a seat at the bar.

A few minutes later, the sheriff came back in, and I was relieved to see that he was alone.

"Is everything okay?" I asked him as he walked past my station at the door.

"No, I've got a hunch that it's not okay at all, but there's not much that I can do about it. Would you mind bringing me a cup of coffee, too?"

"I'd be delighted. Thanks for handling that."

The sheriff just shook his head. "All I did was postpone the inevitable. Have you seen Wayne over at the garage? He's got a black eye that must be killing him, but he wouldn't tell me where he got it."

"I know," I said.

"Yeah, so do I, now."

I got the sheriff his coffee, but it was clear that he wanted some time alone with Robert, so I walked over to Ellen and joined her as she bussed one of the tables. "Are you okay?"

"No, I'm furious," she said. Her hands were still shaking, and I could see that she had a white-knuckle grip on a poor fork that hadn't done anything to her. "He's got some nerve coming in here and demanding my children."

"Don't worry. He won't win."

"You heard him, Victoria. He's got a bank of lawyers now that he's with a rich woman. I'm going to lose my kids if I don't do something drastic. I just know it."

"Slow down. That's not going to happen. We'll enlist

Rebecca to make sure of it." Rebecca Davis was my best friend, and a superb attorney at law. While she didn't take an active part in my unofficial investigations, she was wonderful company, and someone I cherished.

"You can't promise that, and you know it." There was an air of defeat in her words, and I knew that this must have been killing her. Ellen had gone all that time without running into her ex-husband, but now he was back, and with a vengeance.

"You're right. That was out of line. But I can promise you that Rebecca will fight to the death to make sure you don't lose your kids. You're a great mom, Ellen. No judge is going to take your children away from you."

"It happens every day, and you know it. I've got to *do* something."

"Just promise me that you won't do anything crazy," I said.

Ellen shook her head, and I decided that it was time to change the subject. Maybe it would help lighten her mood a little. "So, what's going on with Wayne? I didn't even know that you two were officially seeing each other, and now I hear that he's defending your honor."

"He's a real sweetheart," she said as her stern expression softened. "I didn't want to say anything about it before. I'm sorry, but I didn't want to jinx it. You know my track record with men. I don't have a very good history of choosing the right ones."

"You've got a winner there, though," I said. "Wayne's a good guy."

"Believe me, I know," she said. "He's embarrassed that Gordon got the best of him last night, and he swore that the next time they ran into each other, the outcome would be different. Victoria, what am I going to do about this mess?"

"I'm not sure there's anything that you *can* do at the moment," I said. "Things might just have to run their course."

"If that happens, then, I've already lost."

I hated the air of defeat in her voice, but there was nothing else that I could say.

"Ellen, would you like to go home early today? I can manage here on my own until Jenny comes in at four."

"Thanks, but the kids don't get out of school for hours yet. If you don't mind, I'd rather just stay here and work. Who knows? Maybe it will help take my mind off of things."

"It couldn't hurt, right? If you need anything, you know that all you have to do is ask."

"I know, and I'm sorry I kept this all from you."

"Hey," I said with a grin. "You don't owe me anything but your undying loyalty and friendship. That's not asking too much, is it?"

"Not if you're willing to return it," Ellen said with the first smile I'd seen that day.

"You know it," I said, and we tried to go about our business, despite what had just happened.

Five minutes later, Robert Hightower whispered something to his daughter, and then he walked out of the diner a much calmer man.

As the sheriff paid their bill, I asked, "What did you say to him?"

"I basically told him not to do anything stupid that he'd regret for the rest of his life."

"And what did he say to that?"

The sheriff frowned for a moment before he answered. "That's what I'm worried about. He said if he did something, there wasn't a chance on earth that he'd ever regret it. I don't like it, Victoria. As far as I'm concerned, the sooner Gordon Murphy leaves town, the better."

"As long as he doesn't try to take Ellen's kids with him when he goes, I couldn't agree with you more," I replied.

After the sheriff was gone, I wondered just what Gordon's game was. He'd shown no interest in his children before now, so why the sudden change of heart? Was it his motivation to get them back, or was it his fiancée's? Either way, I had a hunch that things were going to get bad before they got better.

I just hoped that nobody I cared about got hurt in the meantime.

Chapter 2

"What's this I hear about that loser Gordon Murphy showing his face around here this morning?" my grandfather demanded to know as he stormed into the diner an hour later. "Where is he?"

"Take it easy. He's been gone over an hour, Moose," I said. "We managed to throw him out just fine on our own," I added with a smile.

Moose snorted, and then he said, "Fair enough. You know that you can call me if you ever need me, Victoria. We don't have to be investigating a murder for me to lend you a hand."

My grandfather and I had solved a crime or two in the past, and to our mutual surprise, we'd turned out to be quite good at it. Apart from the times our lives were in jeopardy, we enjoyed the thrill of the chase, even when it led us straight into trouble. Well, that was mostly me. I seemed to have a knack for getting myself in difficult situations, but they'd all worked out so far. If we never had to solve another murder as long as we lived, that would be just fine with me, but with our luck, I had a feeling that sooner or later, we'd be called into action again.

"I know you're there for me," I told him as I patted his shoulder. "I'm counting on it, as a matter of fact. Since you're here, why don't you hang around and have a piece of pie?" My grandfather and I both loved pie, just one of many traits and tastes we shared.

"No, I'd better not," he said uncertainly as he shook his head.

I looked at him with justifiable concern. "Moose, are you feeling okay? Should I call a doctor?"

He looked surprised by my new line of questioning. "Why do you ask that? I'm fine, Victoria. I don't want to have anything to do with a doctor, and you know it."

"Normally, I'd agree with you, but let's face it;

something's wrong. You just turned down pie."

My grandfather just shrugged, and then he said with a sheepish smile, "I suppose you're right. After all, what could it hurt?"

"Not a thing in the world, as far as I'm concerned," I said as I reached into the display and brought out the last slice of strawberry pie and grabbed a fork. "Would you like some coffee to go with this?"

"How about some ice cold milk instead?" Moose asked.

"You've got it. I keep some in the back of the fridge, since Greg likes it that way, too." My husband couldn't stand milk that was within shouting distance of merely cool. It had to be cold enough to freeze, and if there happened to be a crust of ice on the top of the glass, he was perfectly fine with that.

After I set Moose up at the counter, he dug into the pie with so much vigor that I considered joining him, despite the fact that I was still working the floor with Ellen.

"Ellen, I hate to complain, but I didn't order this," I heard Reverend Mercer say a few minutes later as Ellen dropped off his plate. As Ellen apologized, the reverend added, "Usually I wouldn't complain, but I'm allergic, you see."

"I'm so sorry. I'll fix it right away," Ellen said as she picked the plate up as though it were toxic. She was clearly off her game; for the first time in a long time, she was getting orders wrong. Even when they were right, she was delivering them to the wrong customers.

I decided that enough was enough, for both our sakes.

"It might not be a bad idea if you go on and head home early," I said as I followed her into the kitchen.

"I don't *want* to leave," Ellen said, though I was having a hard time believing her. She handed the plate to my mother, explained what she'd gotten wrong, and then she turned to me, tears welling up in her eyes. "Maybe you're right. Victoria, I don't know what's gotten into me."

"Come on, don't be so hard on yourself. You're under more strain and pressure than any normal person should have to endure. Go home before the kids get off the bus, take a long hot bath, and turn the ringer off on your phone."

"I couldn't do that," she said.

"Which part?" I asked. "I'm willing to negotiate here," I added with a grin.

"Going home probably isn't a bad idea, and the bath sounds wonderful, but I have kids. I could never turn off my ringer. What if something happened to one of them?"

"Okay, leave your phone on, but the other two items aren't really an option. Go on. Things will look a lot better after a long hot soak."

"You're probably right. After all, I'm not doing much good here. Are you sure you don't mind?"

"I can have Moose drive you, if you'd like him to. I'm sure that he wouldn't mind."

"No, the walk home might help me clear my head. If you're sure, I'm going to take you up on it. Thank you for being there for me, Victoria."

"You're part of our family, Ellen. If there's *anything* I can do, all you have to do is ask."

"Do you mind if I sneak out the back way?" she asked me. "I don't want to be around anyone right now."

"That's fine. I'll see you in the morning, but don't forget, if you need me before then, I'm just a telephone call away."

"I know, and I appreciate it. Bye."

After she left, my mother handed me a new, properly filled plate. As she did, she asked worriedly, "Victoria, is she going to be okay?"

"Honestly, I have no idea. This thing with her ex-husband really has her rattled."

"You did a nice thing sending her home early today," Mom said.

"For us, or for our customers?" I asked with a grin. "After all, she almost killed Reverend Mercer."

"For her," Mom said. "Now, go deliver these orders before they get cold."

"Yes, Ma'am," I said with a soft smile.

I did as my mother suggested, and when I came back over

to Moose, I saw that he'd finished his pie and drained his glass.

"Feel better now?" I asked.

"You were right. Pie never hurts," he admitted as he looked back toward the kitchen. "Is Ellen coming back out soon?" he asked with concern.

"I just sent her home," I said. "She was a wreck."

Moose looked alarmed. "Victoria, you didn't send her out alone, did you?"

"She's a big girl, Moose. She can take care of herself."

"Ordinarily I'd agree with you, but not with that fool of an ex-husband walking around Jasper Fork. She needs someone with her."

"You don't seriously think that she needs to be protected, do you?"

"She's not the one I'm worried about," Moose said as he headed for the back. "What do you think she's going to do if she's worried that Gordon's coming after her children? To be honest, I have a feeling that he's the one who's going to need protection. I personally wouldn't mind one bit if she pushed that weasel into oncoming traffic, but it won't do her kids any good."

Moose was gone before I could stop him, and I wondered if perhaps he was right. Should I have kept Ellen at the diner where she had something to do instead of sending her out on her own? No, I stood by my decision. As far as I was concerned, she needed the peace and quiet of home, not the frenzied activity of the diner.

That didn't keep me from hoping that Moose caught up with her, though. I'd feel better about everything if my grandfather played guardian angel to someone else for a change. It wasn't that I didn't appreciate his thoughtfulness, but sometimes it could be a little much.

Things got busy just then, and I quickly forgot all about Ellen, Gordon, and Moose while I ran the place single-handedly until reinforcements showed up later in the day. It was after one before I thought of Gordon Murphy again, and the only reason he crossed my mind was because his old crony, Sam Jackson, showed up at the diner looking for blood.

"Where is he?" Sam asked as he stormed into the diner. Jackson was a big, hulking man, and his normal expression was a scowl, but the look on his face at the moment took that to a completely different level. I had to do something to calm him down before our customers started fleeing en masse.

"First, you need to lower your voice, and second, you're going to have to be a lot more specific than that, Sam," I said.

He took a deep breath, let it out slowly, and then he said, "Sorry. I know it's not your fault. I heard Gordon Murphy was here."

"He was, a few hours ago, but he's long gone. Why are you so eager to see him?"

"He owes me something, and I mean to get it back."

"I don't think you'll have much problem collecting," I said. "I understand his fiancée is rich."

"This isn't about money. It never was. Do you have any idea where he might be?"

"I can honestly say that I don't have a clue," I replied.

"Don't worry. I'll find him, and when I do, he'll be sorry that he ever came back to town."

Sam left, and I had to smile at the thought of him catching up with Ellen's ex-husband. It sounded as though Gordon was going to be on the wrong end of bullying this time, which would be a nice change of pace. I was still thinking about that when Mitchell Cobb handed me his check, along with a ten-dollar bill.

"Is it true?" he asked me as I made change for him.

"What's that?"

"Is Gordon Murphy really back in town?"

"Do you want to get even with him, too, Mitchell?" I asked. The man was about Ellen's age, and a calmer fellow I'd never met. Mitchell was the original 'Go Along, Get Along' guy.

"He stole Ellen from me a long time ago," Mitchell said in

a hurt voice. "I asked her to the prom, and she said yes, but then Gordon swooped in, and I never had a chance. She's going to be really upset when she finds out that he's back."

"You don't know the half of it," I said. "He already came in here threatening to take her kids away from her, and Ellen doesn't know what she's going to do. I'm sorry that she ditched you for the prom. You must have been upset about it."

"It wasn't her fault," he said with the hint of a soft smile. "Gordon had that effect on people back then. He could charm the pants off a rattlesnake, you know?"

"I don't believe that I've ever seen a snake wearing pants," I said, smiling back.

"You know what I mean."

"I do."

"I don't like that he's here again, not one little bit," Mitchell said.

"You're clearly not the only one upset about it," I said. "Not many folks seem to be pleased that he's back. Have a nice day."

"You, too. Tell Ellen that I'm pulling for her."

"I'm sure she'll appreciate it," I said as I touched his arm lightly.

"What was that all about?" my husband, Greg, asked me as I stepped back in the kitchen for a second.

"What do you mean?"

"First Sam comes blasting in here, and then you have a powwow with Mitchell Cobb. Does he have a problem with Gordon, too?"

"How could you possibly know that from where you were standing, Greg? Mitchell never even raised his voice."

"He didn't have to. For a second there, he had an expression on his face that was pure hatred."

"I didn't see it," I admitted. "Are you sure you read him right?"

"Hey, I'm just a guy working the grill. You're the one with the massive detective skills," he said as he winked at me.

"You have more value than your work with a spatula around here, and you know it," I answered. I would have said more, but just then, Polly Ward approached the register with her check. "Duty calls."

"You know where I am if you need me," Greg said.

"It's what makes me keep smiling throughout the day," I replied.

Things were mostly quiet for the rest of day, and I thought that we might just weather this particular storm, but two minutes before closing, Sheriff Croft came in with a serious expression on his face.

"Where's Ellen?" he asked without even saying hello to me or anyone else.

"She normally leaves the diner at two every afternoon, but I let her off early today. You know as well as I do that there's a lot going on right now, and she needed some time to cope with it all. Why are you looking for her?"

The sheriff frowned as he looked straight at me and said, "I don't know how to tell you this, but she's one of my lead suspects. Somebody just killed Gordon Murphy."

Chapter 3

"What? How did it happen?" I asked as leaned back against the counter.

"It appears that somebody clubbed him in the back of the head with a pipe in the alley between the hardware store and the knitting shop," the sheriff said. "We haven't found the murder weapon yet, but there's no doubt that was what was used to kill him. I'd tell you to keep that part to yourself, but I've got a hunch that it's going to get out fast enough without your help. I went to Ellen's place, but she and her kids were gone."

I couldn't believe she'd just take off like that. "Did you check at her mother's place?"

"I called Opal, but no one answered," the sheriff said. Ellen's folks had separated years ago, but they'd never gone through with their divorce. They were perfectly amicable, aside from the fact that they lived in different houses across the street from each other. It turned out that they enjoyed being together; they just had no taste for living under the same roof. It was an odd solution to their problem, but folks around town had mostly gotten used to it.

"Did you try Robert?"

"No one picked up there, either."

"I'm sure there's a perfectly innocent explanation for it," I said.

The sheriff shook his head. "I hope you're right, but I kind of doubt it. If Ellen were to run, where would she go? Victoria, you're not betraying any trusts here. I need to find her."

"I wish I could help. If she's not at Opal's or Robert's, I don't have a clue, and that's the truth."

"I'll drive over to Opal's right now," the sheriff said as he started for the door. "Victoria, if you talk to her before I do, tell her she needs to find me, and pronto."

"She didn't kill him, Sheriff," I said, but he didn't respond one way or the other as he hurried out the front door of the diner.

Greg whistled softly behind me. "That's bad, isn't it?"

"It couldn't be much worse," I admitted as I reached for my telephone.

"Who are you calling?" Greg asked.

"I need to get a hold of Moose. We have to find out who killed Gordon Murphy."

As I dialed the number, I saw that Greg was studying me with a pained expression. "What is it?" I asked as Moose answered.

"How should I know?" my grandfather asked. "You're the one who called me."

"Get over to the diner," I ordered my grandfather. "Somebody killed Gordon Murphy, and the police don't have a clue as to where Ellen might be."

"I'm on my way," Moose said as he ended the call.

After I hung up, I turned back to Greg. "What's up?"

"I'm worried, that's all," Greg said.

"There's more to it than that, and we both know it."

"Victoria, there's something that you've got to consider. What are you going to do if Ellen *did* kill the man?" he asked softly. "Can you turn over the evidence to the police and let them arrest her? Maybe you and your grandfather should just sit this one out."

"Do *you* think that she's guilty?" I asked Greg calmly.

"Of course not, but you told me yourself how angry she was earlier. She threatened him in broad daylight, Victoria. Even you have to admit that it's possible that Ellen might have killed her ex-husband, not that anyone could blame her if she had."

"I don't believe for one second that she did it," I said.

"But what if you're wrong?" my husband asked me.

"Then we'll put the diner up as collateral if we have to and get her the best attorney we can find. Are you okay with that?"

"It's fine by me," Greg said. "I just don't want to see you get hurt."

I patted his cheek. "I know you don't."

"Just to set the record straight, I really don't think Ellen did it," he added softly.

"I know that, too. You're just looking out for me."

"It can be a full-time job sometimes," he said with a wry grin.

"I can only imagine," I said, matching his smile with one of my own. "She didn't do it, Greg. I know it with all of my heart."

"I hope you're right. There's just one thing, though."

"What's that?" I asked him.

"It would have been a whole lot better if she hadn't run."

I nodded slightly. "I have to agree with you there."

Chapter 4

"I got here as fast as I could," Moose said as he rushed into the diner a few minutes later.

I glanced at my watch. "I can't believe you didn't get a speeding ticket racing over here," I answered.

"Me, either," he said with a sheepish grin. "The cops must all be out looking for Ellen. Any idea where she might have gone?"

"If she's not at Opal's, I don't have a single idea," I said.

"That's where we can start, then," he said as he looked back at the door. "Where is that confounded woman, anyway?"

"That's what we're all trying to figure out," I said.

"Not her. I'm talking about Martha. She was right behind me."

My grandmother walked into the diner at a much more sedate pace. "Moose, one of these days you're going to kill us both. You know that, don't you?"

"I don't drive *that* fast," Moose protested.

"It's not just the speed, it's the maneuvering you do, too."

"Woman, I haven't had a wreck in forty years, and you know it."

Martha raised one eyebrow. "That might be true, but what we don't know is how many accidents you may have caused yourself because of your driving habits." She turned to me and smiled. "Hello, Victoria. I understand you could use a hand."

"That would be great," I said. "I appreciate you coming in on such short notice."

"Nonsense, it's always my pleasure. I enjoy working with your husband. He's got a deft touch with the grill, doesn't he?"

"I like to think so," I said.

"Enough with the pleasantries," Moose snapped. "Let's go, Victoria."

"Lead the way," I answered, and I followed Moose out of the diner. As we got into his truck, I asked, "Do you have any ideas where *else* we might look? The sheriff is on his way to Opal's place." I glanced at my watch. "In fact, he's probably already there."

"Maybe we shouldn't be focused on finding Ellen first, then," Moose said as he started the truck.

"Why wouldn't we? Isn't that our top priority?"

My grandfather shook his head. "Finding out who killed Gordon Murphy should be our only aim, don't you think? Let the police track Ellen down. They have the resources, and besides, while they're searching for her, we can start working on our investigation."

"I don't know," I said, the hesitation clear in my voice.

Moose turned the truck engine off. "Then we won't do anything until we can both agree on a game plan."

"Well, we can't just sit here," I said.

"Tell me where to drive, and I'll be happy to comply."

I thought about it, and after a few moments of thought, I realized that Moose was right. If we spent our time looking for Ellen, we wouldn't be doing anything to advance our investigation. Besides, even if we did manage to find her, all we could do was turn her over to the sheriff, and was that something I really wanted to do?

"Okay, you're right. Ellen's on her own at the moment. How should we start looking into Gordon Murphy's murder?"

"I'd say we should talk to the fiancée first, don't you?"

"What makes you think we can find her, let alone convince her to talk to us about Gordon?" I asked my grandfather.

"She has to be somewhere nearby, since they've been staying in town. Where would you think she and Gordon would stay, since they evidently have plenty of money?"

"It has to be The Harbor Inn, doesn't it?"

"I would think so," Moose said as he started his truck again and drove toward the edge of town where the nicest place anywhere near Jasper Fork was located. The Harbor was the main location in our area where folks held weddings, showers, and all kinds of joyous festivities. Greg and I had only eaten at the restaurant on three occasions in the past, and I didn't see number four happening anytime soon. We'd had to nearly mortgage the house to afford dining there the last time, and staying as a guest of the inn was out of the question.

"Even if she's there, how are we going to get in to see her?" I asked.

"Don't worry about that. I know someone on the inside at The Harbor. If she's there, we'll figure the rest of it out."

"I wish *I* had your faith in us," I said with the hint of a smile.

"You know what they say, fake it 'til you make it. The place is really snazzy, isn't it?" Moose asked as the hotel/restaurant complex came into view. I was amazed that such an elegant place was right in our backyard, but someone clearly had money when they'd built it.

"It's pretty cool. Who's your contact there?" I asked.

"Never you mind. I'm going to drop you off at the lobby. Wait for me there."

I looked at my clothes, and I was painfully aware of the common nature of my blue jeans and T-shirt. "Looking like this?"

"What's wrong with the way you look?" Moose asked.

"Nothing, if I'm going to be cleaning the rooms."

"Oh, you're dressed much too casually for that," my grandfather replied.

"Then how am I going to get away with lounging around in the lobby?"

"Maybe you've got a point," Moose said. "Fine, you can come with me, but I'd appreciate it if you'd let me do the talking."

"What kind of contact do you have here?" I asked. My

grandfather's sphere of influence in our area was much broader than mine, and I couldn't help but wonder if we were going to call on the head honcho. "Who are we talking to, the hotel's general manager?"

"Why on earth would we want to talk to him? He's a stuffed shirt who rarely leaves his office, from everything I've heard about the man. No, we're going to the person with the real power, the only one who knows everything that goes on behind the scenes."

We pulled up around the back to the service entrance, and Moose parked the truck off to one side. "Remember, let me handle this."

"With pleasure," I said.

There was a skinny young man in a bellman's uniform lounging in back flirting with one of the maids, and it surprised me when Moose walked directly up to him.

"Cal, do you have a second?" Moose asked him cordially.

"Sure thing, Captain," Cal said as he lingered long enough to say good-bye to the housekeeper. "What can I do for you?"

"I'm looking for a woman named Jessie."

Before Moose could say another word, the man nodded. "She's in the Hickory Suite, checked in with one Gordon Murphy. The lady prefers bubble baths, cashews, and romance novels. The man's not much of a reader, but he spends a great deal of time on his cellphone. What else do you need?"

I was a little surprised by the bellman's instant recitation. "Pardon me, but how could you possibly know all of that?"

Cal looked at me a few moments, and then he studied Moose. "I'm assuming that she's with you, is that right?"

"Cal, this is my granddaughter, Victoria," Moose said.

Cal nodded. "Pleased to meet you. Ma'am, I make it a point to know about *all* of the guests who stay with us here at The Harbor Inn."

"It sounds a bit invasive to me," I said, not meaning to sound so judgmental.

If Cal took offense, he didn't show it. "Okay, think about it this way. One of my jobs here is to see to our guests' every need, at least the ones we're allowed to provide for them," he added with a smile. "Take Ms. Blackstone's nut preference. I keep the closest pantry to her room well stocked in case she runs out of something in the middle of the night."

"Even romance novels?" I asked with a smile.

"You'd better believe it. I keep a selection on hand, as many of our guests like to read a little for guilty pleasure. The reason I know that is because they rarely take the books with them when they leave us. As for Mr. Murphy's telephone usage, I keep chargers nearby that fit most every phone ever made, just in case one's needed. Knowing their habits and preferences is the *only* way to ensure that our guests get the treatment they're paying for. For them, privacy is a price they are willing to pay for good service."

"But surely they count on your discretion as well," I said.

"Victoria," Moose said a little impatiently. "Cal is talking to us as a favor to me. You understand that, don't you?"

"I'm sorry," I said quickly. "I didn't mean any offense by it."

"I didn't take any, so don't worry about it. If you'd asked me anything without having your grandfather in tow, you wouldn't even have gotten my name, rank, and serial number out of me. It just so happens that I owe Moose a pretty huge favor, and this won't even begin to pay it back."

"Cal, I wiped that slate clean a long time ago," Moose said mysteriously.

"You might have, but I know I still owe you, and until we're even, all you have to do is ask."

"Could I ask you one more thing, then? Do you happen to know if Ms. Blackstone is in her room right now?" Moose asked.

"She went for a walk ten minutes ago, as a matter of fact," Cal said. He pointed to a path near the water and added, "If you head off that way, you're sure to catch up with her."

"Thanks, Cal," Moose said. "We really are even now."

"Not until I say we are," Cal said. "Now if you'll excuse me, I'm due to walk Jimikens for Mrs. Nance. If I'm late, old Jim takes it out on me."

After Cal was gone and Moose and I started down the path that skirted the lake, I asked, "What on earth did you ever do for Cal?"

"That's between us, young lady. What happened to you holding your tongue back there?"

I laughed. "Come on, Moose. We both knew that wasn't going to happen. He really laid it all out there, didn't he? It's clear he feels beholden to you."

"Cal just had a bit of bad luck in the past."

"Why do I have the feeling that it's not as simple as all of that?" I asked.

"I don't have any idea what you're talking about," Moose said as he added a quick wink. "Now, do you have any ideas about how we should approach the grieving fiancée?"

"Well, it's going to be hard to commiserate with her, since she's probably the only person around here who's all that sorry to see something happen to Gordon."

"Maybe so, but she must have seen *something* in him to agree to marry the man," Moose said.

"We can offer our sympathies and go from there," I said.

"I suppose that it's as good a plan as any," my grandfather said.

We never had the chance to implement it, though.

We were about to round a corner when I heard a single voice speaking. It was a woman, and she sounded extremely upset. "I don't know. He wouldn't tell me. No, I don't think he was bluffing. He had something he said would bury me. Yes, I know. It was a poor choice of words, but that's what he told me. No, I can't come back until I find out. Good bye."

I tried to pull Moose back as the conversation ended, but we didn't quite manage it. A rather plain woman in her thirties came down the path, and before she spotted us, there was a dark frown on her lips. She was well dressed, a little too nice for a hike around the lake, and her hair was expensively styled. Before she spotted us, I took a gamble and said to my grandfather, "I'm telling you, we're lost. I have no idea where she is."

Jessie Blackstone and I made eye contact, and I did my best to smile at her as I said, "Are you by any chance Jessie? My grandfather and I had just about given up all hope of finding you out here."

"I'm Jessie Blackstone," she said a little warily. "Why were you looking for me?"

"We knew Gordon," Moose said. "We wanted to come by and offer you our condolences."

"Thank you," she said automatically, though it did nothing to alleviate her scowl. "Excuse me for being so abrupt, but who exactly are you?"

"Forgive me," I said as I stepped forward and offered her my hand. "I'm Victoria Nelson, and this is my grandfather, Moose."

She started to reach out her hand automatically before she heard my name, but as I said it, Jessie pulled it back as though we were a pair of vipers. "You own that awful diner," she said.

"I wouldn't call it awful," Moose said, using his most charming smile. "We prefer to call it quaint, if you don't mind."

"It's where that woman works, though," she said.

"Which woman are you referring to?" I asked, though I knew full well who she meant.

"Gordon's ex-wife, Ellen. She wouldn't let him see his own children. Can you imagine anyone being so cruel?"

"Hang on a second," I said, trying to keep my voice calm. "You don't know the entire situation. Gordon left her high and dry to raise two kids all alone. You can't really blame her for not welcoming him back to town with open arms, can you?"

"I understand that sometimes people have differences in a marriage, but when Gordon first told me about his children, I could barely believe it. He assured me that when he left, he did his best to stay in their lives, but she wouldn't allow it."

"Let me guess. *You're* the one who insisted that he come back to Jasper Fork and fight for them, aren't you?"

Jessie nodded a little uncertainly. "It was the right thing to do. I could never have married him without at least meeting his children. What kind of man doesn't see his own offspring?"

"Was trying to get custody your idea as well?" Moose asked.

"He needed to be a part of their lives, and we could afford to give them the very best things," Jessie said. "Don't they deserve that much, after what they'd been through?"

"They don't deserve losing their mother," I said, and I could barely contain my feelings. Ellen was the greatest mother in the world as far as I was concerned, putting the welfare of her children above her own every step of the way.

"Of course they don't," Jessie said, and I believed her. "It was never my intention for us to seek full custody."

"Ellen believed otherwise," I said.

Jessie frowned. "I *told* Gordon that it was a foolish strategy, but he believed that if we threatened to seek full custody, Ellen would be more compliant about allowing us into their lives."

"I don't suppose any of it matters now," I said.

Jessie looked off toward the lake. "No, I suppose that it doesn't. Have the police found her yet?"

"Ellen?" Moose asked. "How did you know that they were looking for her?"

"Sheriff Croft came here and spoke to me," Jessie said. "Naturally, I told him about the argument Gordon had last night in Ellen's home, and he left in search of your waitress."

"Where were *you* when it happened?" I asked her.

Jessie looked away again before she spoke. "I don't suppose we should be talking about it, since it's part of an ongoing murder investigation."

"What would it hurt for you to give us your alibi?" Moose asked. "It might make things easier for you if we could eliminate you as a suspect right off the bat."

Jessie looked startled by the thought that Moose and I would be involved in searching for Gordon Murphy's killer. "What possible business is it of yours?"

"My grandfather and I have been known to help the police out from time to time," I said. I wasn't exactly sure that Sheriff Croft would put it that way, but it was still true.

"I didn't realize that either one of you had any official status," Jessie said.

"It's more of an informal thing," I said.

Jessie shook her head. "Then I'll deal with the sheriff directly. Now, if you'll excuse me, I'm afraid that this tragedy has taken quite a toll on me."

As she headed past us on the path, Moose and I turned to follow her. We took a dozen steps nearly in tandem when Jessie whirled around and faced us. "Are you honestly going to follow me?" There was real anger in her expression, and I was glad that Moose was with me, despite the fact that I had at least twenty pounds on this woman.

"It's the only way back to the inn," I said.

She stared at us for a few seconds more, shook her head, and then she stormed on, doing her best to ignore us.

I touched Moose's arm to hold him back a little, but he just shrugged, so we walked on together.

When Jessie got back to open ground, her pace increased, and she was soon stomping off toward the safety of her hotel.

"She's a little touchy about her alibi, isn't she?" Moose asked. "I thought for a second there that she was going to push us both off the path straight into the lake."

"I understand her being a little on edge," I said. "After all, someone just killed her fiancé."

"Was it me, or did she not seem too upset about who might have done it?" I asked.

"What do you mean?"

"She didn't show much grief, as far as I'm concerned. She was angry, and more than a little defensive, but not grieving. And what about that telephone call we overheard? I wonder who she could have been talking to."

"I don't have a clue," Moose said as he scratched his chin. "We need to keep an eye on her. I'm automatically suspicious of anyone who refuses to share their alibis with us, aren't you?"

"Not everyone has one," I said.

"No, but she sidestepped the question the second she heard it. I've got a hunch that she's hiding something."

"Do you think she killed him?" I asked my grandfather.

"It's something we can't rule out, but I have to wonder about something. If she *is* guilty, what made her get rid of him right here and now? She's really the only one who's been a part of Gordon's life lately, so why kill him once he's back in a town where he made a great many enemies?"

"That's the answer to your question right there," I said.

"I don't follow you," Moose answered.

"What better place to bump him off than someplace where there are half a dozen other viable suspects? If she planned it that way, she's absolutely brilliant."

"And if she didn't?"

"Then she's pretty gutsy, or maybe she's just an innocent bystander." I hesitated, and then I added, "The only time I bought her completely was when she was talking about Ellen's kids. I've got a hunch that she was sincere about that, and Gordon knew it. His kids were a deal-breaker for her, and he must have really wanted her money. Why else would he risk coming back here after all of these years not knowing what he was going to face?"

"Knowing Gordon, the potential profit had to outweigh the danger."

I was about to reply when I looked up and saw that Cal was walking toward us, along with a pair of husky men wearing sharp-looking suits.

None of them were smiling, and I had to wonder if this was more bad news for us.

Chapter 5

"I'm afraid you two are going to have to leave the premises," Cal said as he reached us first. "We can't have you walking the grounds upsetting our guests."

"Who exactly has been complaining about us?" Moose asked. He was clearly in no mood to comply with exiting the property without a fight.

"This is private property, sir," one of the men said, clearly from the security team. "We don't need to provide any information other than that. Now, if you'll tell us what you're driving, we'll be happy to escort you to your vehicle."

"What if we came by for lunch?" I asked as I pointed to the restaurant.

"I'm sorry, but that's not going to work. We're booked for the foreseeable future."

Moose looked at Cal, who seemed to shrug for just a second. It was clear that this wasn't his idea, but there was nothing he could do about it, especially since he'd been the one who'd told us where we'd find Jessie in the first place. "We're truly sorry," he said, though it was clear by his tone that he was doing his best to match his companions' tone.

"No worries," Moose said with a grin that was clearly artificial. At least it was clear to me. "We're off, then. No hard feelings."

No one responded to that, so my grandfather and I walked back to his truck with an escort. As I started to get in the passenger side, I looked over at the restaurant and saw one of the drapes flutter. Someone had been watching the entire procession, and I had a good hunch who that might be. Well, at least we'd given Jessie a show to go along with her meal.

As we pulled out of the parking lot, I said, "Wow, that was fast, wasn't it? They didn't waste any time getting rid of us."

Moose just shrugged. "When there's that kind of money involved, I'm pretty sure the hotel staff is ready to do just about anything that they're called on to do."

"Still, you gave up pretty easily," I said with a grin. "What happened, did their sheer numbers intimidate you into backing down?"

"Yeah, that was it entirely," Moose said, matching my smile. "I knew that we weren't going to get anything else out of Jessie today, so it was important that no one had to actually throw us off the property. This way we're free to come back and speak with her again later."

"Do you honestly think that's going to happen?"

"You never know," Moose said. "Who should we tackle next?"

"I say we go by the garage and have a little chat with Wayne," I said. "It sounds as though he had a few reasons of his own to take a pipe to the back of Gordon Murphy's head. Not only did the man punch his lights out, but he did it in front of his girlfriend. I've got the feeling that more than Wayne's pride was hurt by that blow."

"Do you think it was enough to make him kill Gordon?" Moose asked.

"If he thought he was defending Ellen, it might be," I said.

"Then by all means, let's go speak with him while the sheriff's occupied with his search for Ellen."

"Surely he's found her by now," I said.

"That depends entirely on how good she is at hiding," Moose replied.

"I still can't believe that she'd just run off like that."

"Fight or flight is pretty ingrained in all of us," my grandfather answered.

"I just hope that she didn't do both," I answered as we pulled into the auto shop's parking lot.

It was time to talk to the owner and see if he might have had something to do with Gordon Murphy's murder.

"Wayne, do you have a second?" Moose asked him as we walked into the office.

"For you? Always," the mechanic said.

Moose whistled softly under his breath when he saw the mechanic's face. "Gordon caught you pretty good last night, didn't he?"

Wayne frowned as he touched his black eye. He winced a little as he did, and then he looked straight at Moose and said, "I've never been much of a fighter, and that's a fact. Before this happened, the last time I raised a hand in anger was in seventh grade, and that didn't end all that well for me either, truth be told. The man hit me before I was ready, but that's not much of an excuse, is it?"

"Why did he take a swing at you?" I asked.

"I objected to his tone of voice," Wayne said. "I know that he and Ellen have their differences, but I was going to be whelped if I stood there and let him talk to her that way. I told him to take it easy, and he hit me. That's when he made a mistake."

"What did he do?" Moose asked.

"He thought he'd whipped me and that I wasn't going to get back up. He was wrong. I got a good shot into his gut before he hit me again. I'm not all that proud of it, but it felt good dishing out a little punishment to him."

"What broke things up?" I asked.

"Ellen stepped in between us," Wayne said. "I wasn't all that happy about it at the time, but I should probably thank her for doing it. Most likely I would have gotten clobbered a lot worse than I did if she hadn't," he said with the hint of a smile.

"Wayne, were you mad enough to kill him when you two were fighting?" I asked.

"I know I shouldn't admit it, but yes, if I'd had something I could have used as a weapon, I probably would have taken care of him once and for all."

"You know that he's dead, don't you?" Moose asked.

"Yeah, I know," he said, the words escaping in a sigh. "Sheriff Croft came by looking for Ellen earlier. I didn't know where she could have gone. Has she turned up yet?"

"Not that we know of," I said. "I'm kind of surprised that

you aren't out looking for her yourself."

Wayne scowled as he said, "I was going to do just that, but the sheriff warned me that I needed to stay right where I was until he found her. I thought about disobeying him, but then I realized that even if I did manage to track Ellen down, she wouldn't go to the sheriff on my say-so. That woman has a cast iron backbone, doesn't she?"

"Yes, she can be decisive at times," I said.

That brought a laugh from Wayne. "I suppose that's one way to put it. I keep hoping that she'll call me, but so far, I haven't heard a word from her. To be honest with you, it is kind of hurting my feelings a little. Victoria, if you took off, wouldn't Greg be the first call you made?"

"That's different," I said. "We've been married a long time."

"I don't know," Wayne said. "I still think that she should have called me. Doesn't she realize that she can count on me? I'm in it, the good *and* the bad."

Moose put a hand on Wayne's shoulder. "Don't be too hard on her, son. She's been through a lot, and she honestly believes that her children are at risk. She's not thinking straight right now."

Wayne nodded after a moment's thought. "I suppose you're right. Where could she be, though?"

"If we had a clue between us, we'd go looking for her," I said. "Instead, we're trying to figure out who killed Gordon Murphy."

A light seemed to switch on behind Wayne's eyes. "Is that why you're here, then? Do you two honestly think that I did it?"

"We're talking to everyone who had a problem with the man," I said. "You have to admit that you fit in that category."

"I suppose that I have to," Wayne said. "Just for the record, I didn't kill him. I can't say I didn't consider it, but it passed pretty quickly. If he'd attacked Ellen physically, or if he'd come after me with something more substantial than his fists, maybe I'd do it in the heat of the moment, but not cold-blooded like that."

"What makes you think that hitting him in the head with a steel pipe is spontaneous?" Moose asked him.

"From what I heard, he got smacked in the *back* of the head. That means that someone waited until he turned his back, or else they ambushed him from the shadows. Either way, it was an act of cowardice, and that's something I would never do."

One of the mechanics came out through the shop and headed straight for Wayne's office. "Boss, do you have a second? I'm having trouble with the brakes on that truck Larry Dale brought in."

"I've worked on that one before," Wayne said. "It's kind of tricky." Wayne turned back to us as he got up from his chair. "Folks, I'd love to sit around and chat with you, but Larry is coming back in an hour for his truck, and I don't want to hear him complaining about my service all over town. If I hear from Ellen, I'll let you know, but that's the best I can do."

"Thanks, Wayne," Moose said. "Listen, we didn't mean anything by questioning you. You know that, don't you?"

Wayne smiled a little. "Moose, I appreciate the gesture, but don't go backpedaling now. I know that your loyalties are with Ellen. If you thought for a second that I killed her ex-husband, you wouldn't hesitate to turn me in to the police, and I wouldn't blame you. She's a part of your family, whether there's blood involved or not. We've been friends for a while, but nothing like that."

"I won't deny it," Moose said as he held onto Wayne's hand. "If you did kill that rat, I won't go out of my way to point it out to the police unless there's no other way to save Ellen."

Wayne grinned broadly. "That's all that I can ask. I'm glad that we understand each other."

"So am I," Moose said.

When we were outside the repair shop getting ready to get into my grandfather's truck, I asked him, "Did you just mean what you told Wayne?"

"I did," Moose said solemnly.

"So if we find the pipe with his bloody fingerprints on it, you're not planning on telling Sheriff Croft," I said, having a hard time believing it even as I spoke.

"Face it, Victoria. The man was a rat," Moose said.

"That doesn't mean that he deserved to die," I answered.

"Maybe not, and if the sheriff catches the man's killer, I won't do anything to stop it, but that doesn't mean that I'll serve him up on a platter, either."

I stood in my tracks as I stared at my grandfather. "Moose, if we find evidence that points to whoever killed Gordon, I'm turning it over to the sheriff, no matter *who* it is."

"Even if it's Ellen?" he asked.

"Yes," I replied.

"What if I did it?" Moose asked. There wasn't a single ounce of kidding in his expression, and I knew that his question was deadly serious.

"And you were dumb enough to leave proof behind?" I asked.

"Let's say that I had a lapse in judgment and panicked," Moose said.

"I'd be crying like a baby, but I'd still turn you in," I said. "I can't be the one who decides who gets punished and who goes free. I'd hate myself for the rest of my life, but it's the only way that I'd be able to live with myself. I'm sorry, but that's just the way that I'm wired."

Moose startled me by hugging me right there in the parking lot. "Victoria, truth be told, I'd expect nothing less from you," he said.

"And you wouldn't hate me for doing it?"

"I might be a little miffed at first," Moose said with a grin, "but I'd have plenty of time to get over it, wouldn't I? Granddaughter, I love you with all of my heart, but we're going to have to agree to disagree about this."

"There's one thing we need to get straight, though. You won't try to stop me if I find evidence about someone we know and I try to turn it in, will you?"

"I said that *I* wouldn't do it, not that *you* couldn't," Moose said. "I won't stand in your way, and that's a solemn promise."

"Then let's keep looking," I said.

Moose glanced at his watch. "It's nearly six o'clock. Who should we go after now?"

"I'd really like to talk to Sam Jackson. He was pretty intent on getting his revenge on Gordon when he came by the diner earlier."

"That's fine with me," Moose said. "Just out of curiosity, is there anyone else we should be talking to?"

"Robert Hightower has to be a candidate in our minds, and Opal, too."

Moose shook his head. "I can see Robert going off in a fit, but Opal?"

"Think about it. How would your wife react if someone went after my dad?"

Moose shuddered visibly. "I wouldn't want to be in the man's shoes. You're right. Opal has to be a candidate as well. Is there anyone else?"

I thought about it, and then I remembered my conversation with Mitchell Cobb. After I told Moose about our conversation, I said, "He seemed a little too wrapped up in Ellen for his own good, if you know what I mean. I've got a hunch that old Mitchell knows how to milk a grudge."

"It sounds a little extreme to me, killing a man because he stole your date for the senior prom several years ago," Moose said.

"Do you think we should take his name off our list?" I respected my grandfather's opinion, even when we disagreed.

"No, we'd better leave it right where it is for now," he said. "It's pretty amazing that Gordon dared show his face in town, given how many folks we've discovered wouldn't mind seeing the man dead."

"He never would have done it if Jessie hadn't insisted that he get involved in his children's lives," I said, "but it sounded like a deal-breaker to her, didn't it?"

"If you want to know the truth, I still think she's a viable candidate," Moose said.

"I don't disagree. I'm just not sure how we're going to manage to interview her again."

"We might have to wait to pounce once she's left the hotel property," Moose said.

I nodded, and then I said, "In the meantime, we should talk to Sam Jackson. Do you have any idea where he might be?"

Moose looked at his watch, and then he said, "Unless I miss my guess, he's at The Hole right about now."

The Hole was officially named The Watering Hole, but nobody called it that. It was across the county line, where liquor by the drink was still legal, and I knew that some folks from town slipped across the line every now and then when they wanted a snort.

"How could you possibly know that?" I asked my grandfather with a grin.

"I may be an old man, but that doesn't mean that I don't know things," Moose said.

"I never doubted it for one second," I said. "So, should we go spend a little time at the bar and see if we can find Sam?"

My grandfather looked a little troubled by my suggestion. "Victoria, why don't I drop you off at the diner first? I can handle this by myself."

"Moose, I shouldn't have to remind you that I'm a grown woman. If I want to go to a bar, there's nobody who can stop me."

"I know that you *can*. I'm just not sure that you *should*."

I had to laugh. "Are you worried about my reputation? Should we wait until Greg can go and offer to chaperone me?"

"No, you're right. I'm just being silly."

I patted his shoulder softly. "You're looking out for me,

and normally I wouldn't have a problem with it, but this isn't one of those times."

Moose shrugged. "Let's go, then, but I'm warning you, if you get yourself in a bar fight, I'm not stepping in to give you a hand."

He was doing his best to make up for the slight offense, and I decided to accept his unspoken apology for treating me like a little girl. "Okay, but I don't know why you'd miss out on all of the fun like that."

"You're right again," Moose said. "If our family goes down, we'll go down swinging."

It was all for naught, though. Against Sam Jackson's usual habits, he wasn't at the bar, and the bartender hadn't seen him when we asked about him.

Was Ellen the only one on the run right now, or had we just lost another of our viable suspects?

Chapter 6

"Where do you suppose he could be?" I asked Moose as we went back out to his truck.

"Well, I doubt that he's with Ellen and her kids," my grandfather said.

"Why would she be with *him*?" I asked.

Moose waved a hand around in the air as though he was shooing away a pesky fly. "She wouldn't. I was just thinking out loud."

"Well, you might want to try curbing that a little," I said. "Somebody might hear you."

"Got it. Should we head back to the diner, or do you want to try tracking Jackson down somewhere else?"

"Let's head over to Opal's place. I'm dying to know if Ellen's there."

"Victoria, you haven't changed your mind about her, have you? Do you honestly think that she's capable of murder?" my grandfather asked. "I've known that woman since she was a little girl, and there's no way that she's a killer."

"*I* know that. I was thinking more about Opal and Robert."

My grandfather shook his head. "Sorry, but I just don't see it. Neither one of Ellen's parents strike me as a murderer."

"Even if it meant protecting their grandchildren from harm?" I asked. "I don't see how we can count Opal or Robert out until we get solid alibis for them."

"This is going to be uncomfortable," Moose said as he took off toward Ellen's mother's house.

"You're not afraid of them, are you?" I asked with the hint of a smile.

"Well, not usually, but you make a good point about what a grandparent might do to protect their fold."

"Don't worry," I said as I patted his arm. "I'll be there to protect you."

"Who's going to look out for you?" Moose asked with a

smile.

"I kind of thought we'd look out for each other," I said.

"You know it," my grandfather said.

As he drove toward Opal's house, I looked out the truck window, wondering where my morning server had gotten herself off to. Where would I run if I had two kids I needed to protect?

"Moose, you didn't loan Ellen your fishing cabin, did you?" I asked.

He looked startled by the question. "No, of course not."

"But you would have done it if she'd asked you, wouldn't you?"

To my grandfather's credit, he didn't even hesitate when he answered me. "Of course I would have."

"There's no chance she knows where you hide the spare key, is there?"

Moose shrugged. "Well, I don't exactly make a secret of it."

"Is it possible that she took her children there?" I asked. "She's been to your cabin before, hasn't she?"

My grandfather nodded. "Remember? I loaned it to her last year for a few nights of R&R. She needed to get away."

"Then she might be there now," I said.

"Let's go see," Moose said.

As he pulled into the park to turn around, I said suddenly, "Forget it. We don't need to go after all."

"Why not? It's a solid theory, Victoria."

"Maybe so, but Ellen's over by the swing set with her kids, and Opal's with them, too."

Moose parked the truck, and we hurried over to them.

Ellen looked a little worried by our sudden appearance. "What's going on?"

"Have you talked to anyone this afternoon or evening?" I asked her.

"No, we've been here since school let out."

"We had a picnic," Ellen's youngest said proudly.

"What fun," I said. "Opal, would you mind taking the kids

for a few minutes? We need to speak with Ellen."

"Of course," she said as she put her knitting away. "Has something happened?"

"Later, Mom," Ellen told her.

"Hey, kids, we have a little duck food in the hamper. Would you like to go over to the water and feed them again?"

That suggestion was a big hit, and as the three of them hurried over to the bend in the creek where the ducks were swimming, Ellen asked, "What happened?"

"Somebody killed Gordon this afternoon," Moose said.

Ellen stared at him as though he were kidding, but when she saw both our faces, she crumpled a little, and Moose stepped in to steady her.

"Let's go sit at that bench over there," Moose said, and we followed him there.

"You look shook up by the news," I told Ellen.

"It's a shock, to hear it," she said. "I haven't loved him for a long time, but that doesn't mean that he wasn't once an important part of my life. He's the father of my children, for goodness sake. What happened? Did they catch the killer?"

"As a matter of fact, the sheriff is out looking for you," Moose said softly.

"I didn't do it," Ellen said. "I was with my kids."

"The whole afternoon? You left work early, so they weren't out of school yet when you left the diner."

"No, not the entire time. I wandered around on my own, spent a little time with Wayne, and then I took the kids to dad's place after school so I could clear my head a little. It didn't work, so I swung by and picked them up, and then we all dropped in on Mom. That's when we decided that we should have a picnic for dinner. We've been here a few hours, but I don't have an alibi for the complete day. What time was he killed?"

"We don't know yet," I said, "but that doesn't mean that the police don't have a time of death narrowed down. You might be fine."

"We both know that I don't have that kind of luck," Ellen

said. "If something happened to Gordon, I'm willing to bet that I won't have an alibi for his time of death. What happened to him, anyway? Was it gruesome?"

"It was probably bad enough," Moose said. "Someone hit him in the back of the head with a steel pipe. If it's any consolation, I've got a hunch that he never even saw it coming."

"Who would hit him from behind?" she asked. "That sounds so cowardly."

"It might have been the only way they could catch him by surprise," Moose said.

"I can't believe that he's dead," Ellen said as she slumped a little forward.

"That means the custody battle is over," I said gently.

"I suppose it does at that, but it also gives me a pretty good motive to want to see him dead, too, doesn't it?"

"You're clearly not the only one in Jasper Fork to wish the man ill," Moose said.

"That's true enough. Oh, no. I have to talk to Wayne."

She started to stand, but I put a hand on her shoulder. "We've already spoken. He knows all about it, and he's worried about you, Ellen."

"He didn't do it, did he? That poor sweet fool probably thought he was protecting me," she said as she grabbed my hand.

I looked into her eyes as I asked, "Ellen, you don't have any reason to believe that Wayne killed him, do you?"

"No. Of course not. That's ridiculous." It was pretty clear that she didn't find it that hard to believe, no matter what she said to the contrary. "I need to see him."

"All in good time," Moose said. "The first thing you need to do is talk to Sheriff Croft. He's focusing all of his resources and energy on you, since it looks as though you ran away."

"I didn't run anywhere," Ellen snapped. "I took a picnic in the park with my kids and my mother. No one can claim I was trying to run away from anything."

"Take it easy. I'm sure the sheriff will keep an open mind once you tell him what happened."

"I don't know if he will. The last time I saw Gordon was at the diner this morning. He was fine when he walked out that door, but how can I prove that I didn't kill him?"

"We'll figure this out. Don't worry," I said as I patted her shoulder.

"You two *are* going to find the killer, aren't you?" she asked my grandfather and me.

"We're going to do our best," I said as I watched her kids feeding the ducks, oblivious to the fact that their father was dead. I would hate to be the one who told them that Gordon had been murdered, but I didn't think the burden should fall on Ellen, either. "Do you want me to tell them about their dad?"

She shook her head. "No, my family and I will handle it, but not here. I don't want them to associate the news about their father with this park. It's their favorite place in the world, and I won't take that from them. Do you understand, Victoria?"

"I get it," I said. "They need to know as soon as possible, though, before they hear it from someone else."

"At least let us get back to my mother's place. They'll feel safe there."

"You can probably delay that, but you can't put off that call to the sheriff," I said.

"I won't," she answered. "Mom's place is two blocks away. Surely it can wait until then."

"Okay. Why don't you all hop into the back of Moose's truck, and we can drive over there together?"

"No offense, but I don't feel as though it's all that safe for them riding in back," Ellen said.

"Then they can ride up front with me," Moose said, "if you don't mind sitting in back with Victoria and your mother."

"Thanks for the offer, but we'll walk. It's not far, and it's how we got here in the first place."

I thought about what it might mean if the sheriff saw all of us heading over there together before anyone decided to call him. "That sounds like a good plan. As a matter of fact, we'll walk with you," I said.

"We will?" Moose asked.

"I will, at any rate. You can meet us there, if you'd like."

"No, I can come back later for my truck," my grandfather said.

"Then it's settled," I said as I put my arm around Ellen. "Let's get your gang and head back."

We approached Opal and the kids, and Ellen said, "There are homemade cookies Grandma made for you back at her house. Who wants a cookie?"

There were delighted yelps, and we headed down the sidewalk toward Opal's. Ellen tugged her mother's sleeve and pulled her back a little, so Moose and I took responsibility for the kids as we walked together. Opal stopped for a second, and then caught herself when Ellen must have told her the news.

"Are you okay?" I heard Opal ask her daughter, and Ellen nodded solemnly.

"That's all that matters, then," Opal said.

We were nearly to Opal's house when I saw a squad car parked in front as we walked around the corner. I'd been afraid of that, so I already had a plan.

"Ellen, call the sheriff right now."

"We're almost there," she protested as she looked at her kids. "Surely it can wait two minutes."

"I don't think so," I said as I pointed to the police car. "Kids, hang on one second. Mom, take their hands."

"What's going on?" Ellen's oldest asked.

"I have to make a quick telephone call," Ellen explained.

"Sheriff, I understand you're looking for me," she said once she got him on the phone.

"Where are you?" I could hear the sheriff's harsh question through the telephone.

"I'm at my mother's place, or at least I will be in two

minutes."

"Where have you been all afternoon?" he asked as we all watched him get out of his squad car.

"We had a picnic," she said as she hung up the phone.

The sheriff gave me an icy look the second he saw me, and then it softened into a smile when he looked at Ellen's kids. "Why don't you all go inside? I need to talk to your mother."

"What happened?" one of Ellen's kids asked the sheriff.

"Come inside," Opal said. "There are cookies waiting for you, remember?"

"Cookies," they both shouted, and soon enough, the sheriff was forgotten.

"We need to talk," the sheriff told Ellen.

"Not without Rebecca," I said.

"You already have a lawyer?" Sheriff Croft asked her critically.

"She didn't before, but she does now," I said.

"I don't mind talking to him alone, Victoria," Ellen said.

"See? She's trying to cooperate," Sheriff Croft said. "Don't make this more difficult than it has to be."

"No offense, Sheriff, but it will be as hard as it needs to be."

I called Rebecca, who agreed to come right over.

After I hung up, I said, "She'll be here in five minutes."

"Then, you can tell her to meet us in my office," Sheriff Croft said.

"Are you arresting me?" Ellen asked incredulously.

"Not just yet. We're going to my office to make things a little easier to control," the sheriff said.

"Should I go with him?" Ellen asked me.

"You don't have any choice," the sheriff said bluntly. "That wasn't a request, Ellen; it was an order."

"We'll send Rebecca to you," I said. "Don't worry, and don't say a thing until she gets there."

Ellen nodded, but it was clear that she was scared. I didn't blame her. I'd been the central suspect in a murder investigation before, and I hadn't liked it one bit either. "Rebecca will be there soon."

"Tell Mom to watch the kids," Ellen said as the sheriff put her in his squad car. At least she got to ride up front with him, and not in the back.

"Change of plans," I told Rebecca. "The chief's taking Ellen to his office."

My best friend chuckled a little. "So, that's the way he wants to play it. You know, I've been itching for a good fight, and it sounds as though this one's all mine."

"She didn't do it," I told Rebecca.

"Don't worry. I'm on board."

After I hung up, I looked at Moose. "Did I do wrong advising her to shut up?"

"It was good advice, no matter how the sheriff reacted to it. Do you want to talk to Opal, or should I?" It was pretty clear that my grandfather had no desire to have that particular conversation, so I decided to let him off the hook.

"Tell you what. Why don't you go get the truck, and by the time you get back, I'll be finished talking to her."

He didn't even hesitate when he heard my suggestion. "Done." He nearly sprinted back down the sidewalk toward the park. I turned, took a deep breath, and headed inside to talk to Opal.

At least the kids were occupied. Opal had parked them in front of the television, and there was a plate of cookies between them.

"Where's Ellen?" Opal asked me softly.

"The sheriff decided that it might be better if they talked downtown," I answered.

"I won't have it, do you hear me?" Opal asked. "Get him back here this instant. I want to confess."

Chapter 7

"You killed Gordon Murphy," I said flatly.

"I did. I lured him into the alley and I got rid of him."

"How did you do it, Opal?"

She frowned, as though she was in a haze. "I don't remember. Why does it matter? I did it."

Evidently Ellen hadn't told her mother just how Gordon had been killed. "I'm sure that Ellen would appreciate you trying to take responsibility for what happened, but you aren't doing her any favors. You know that, don't you?"

"She can't go to jail," Opal said, clearly fighting off tears. "Think about her children."

"Opal, do you think Ellen killed her ex-husband?"

"No, of course not," she said. "Keep your voice down, would you?"

"They'll find out that you confessed to killing their father sooner or later," I replied, though I complied by lowering my voice as I said it. "How is Ellen going to feel when she finds out that you tried to confess to save her? She's going to know that you think she did it."

"I never said that," Opal said loudly, violating her own request. The kids looked up from the screen for a moment before going back to their show.

"Then let's just forget that you just confessed," I said. "Rebecca's looking out for Ellen. You don't have to worry about her."

"I know that she can't afford her services," Opal said. "I've got a little put away. I might be able to pay her."

"Right now she's doing it as a favor to me," I said. "We'll worry about who pays her later, okay? For now, you need to have a talk with the children about their father. Can you do that?"

She looked at them worriedly before she turned back to

me. "I don't want Ellen to have to do it, so I suppose I have to."

The front door opened, and Robert Hightower walked in. "Where have you been, Opal? Was Ellen with you the entire time?"

The kids told their grandfather hello, but their gazes never left the television.

"She's at the police station, Bobby," Opal said.

Ellen's father scowled. "We'll see about that."

I put a hand on his shoulder. "Mr. Hightower, she's in good hands right now. Rebecca Davis is with her, so nothing's going to happen to her. Your wife needs you here right now."

"What's wrong, Opal?" he asked her softly. The two obviously cared deeply about each other, even though they hadn't been able to live in the same house together. Robert hadn't gone far, though, buying the house across the street.

"They have to be told about their father," Opal said, her voice choking a little.

"I'll handle it," Robert said.

"We'll do it together. I'll be right beside you," Opal answered.

"I'll be in touch," I said, not wanting to intrude on this painful family moment.

"Do I need to take you home?" Robert asked as he flexed his right hand a little. It appeared to be giving him a little trouble, and I noticed some fresh bruises on his knuckles.

"What happened to your hand?"

"This? It's nothing," he said.

"It looks like something to me," I said, not willing to let up until I heard the truth.

"I punched a wall, okay? It was stupid, but I was frustrated, and I took it out on the concrete. Not very bright of me, but I don't think anything's broken."

"You might want to have somebody look at that."

"I'm not worried about it. Now, how about that ride?"

"Thanks, but Moose will be out front in a second. We'll

talk later."

"That's fine, then," Robert said, and then he reached down and took his wife's hand in his. "It's time, Opal."

I didn't envy them the conversation they were about to have.

I got into Moose's truck as he stopped in front of the house. "How did it go?"

"Opal and Robert were just about to tell the kids about their father when I walked out the door. It's going to be a bad night for everyone concerned in that family."

"Yes, but it has to be done," Moose said. "Where should we go now?"

I was suddenly exhausted from the day I'd just had. "Would you mind taking me home? I need to see Greg and give him a great big hug."

"I was just thinking the same thing about Martha," he admitted. "Life is short, isn't it?"

"And we're not promised a single extra day of it," I said.

"Is Ellen going to be okay?" Moose asked me as he drove me home.

"Rebecca's looking out for her. I'm hoping that Ellen calls me when they're finished."

"Call me after you hear from her. I don't care what time it is, okay?"

"I promise," I said he pulled into my driveway and I got out of the truck. "Bye."

"Good bye, Victoria," he said.

Greg met me on the porch, and I squeezed him so hard I could feel the breath escaping from his lungs. "Hey, are you okay?"

"I am now," I said, my voice muffled in his chest.

"I made homemade pasta," he said. "Are you hungry?"

"Give me one more minute," I said as I hugged him even harder.

My husband stroked the back of my head gently. "Take all the time you need," Greg said. "I'm not going anywhere."

"I'm holding you to that," I said, and then I finally pulled away.

"Rough day?" he asked me as we walked inside the house.

"I've had better," I said. "Now, what's this about homemade pasta?"

"I was worried about you, and you know how I am when I'm jumpy. I cook. You don't mind, do you?"

"I'll take your pasta any day," I said. "Do you have salad, too?"

"You bet. The water's been boiling for a while. In three minutes, we'll be eating."

"Did you wait for me?" I asked.

"I wasn't about to eat without you."

I took a deep breath, and smiled. "You made garlic bread too, didn't you?"

"I figured you wouldn't mind."

"You figured right."

The food was delicious, and we were cleaning up when my phone rang. "It's Rebecca," I said.

"Go on. I'll take care of this."

I hesitated long enough to kiss him quickly, and then I answered my phone. "Hey, what's up?"

"I'm not interrupting anything, am I?" she asked.

"Nothing that won't wait. How's Ellen?"

"She's free," Rebecca said, "at least for the moment. She gave me permission to catch you up. There's really not much to say. She doesn't have the slightest hint of an alibi for the time of the murder, and Sheriff Croft's not all that pleased with any of us."

"It looks bad, doesn't it?"

"Victoria, I've faced worse prospects in my career, but it's not going to be easy. After all, she had every reason in the world to wish the man harm."

"Do you mind taking the case? I'll pay you whatever it takes."

Rebecca laughed. "Let's not get ahead of ourselves just yet. If, and it's a big if, she's arrested for Gordon's murder, then we'll talk about my fee."

"Rebecca, I don't expect you to do this for free," I said. "Ellen is one of ours at the diner, and we take care of our own."

"I figured as much, but honestly, I haven't done much yet but hold her hand."

"That's worth more than gold to me," I said. "Have I told you how happy I am to have you as a best friend?"

"I don't mind hearing it again," she said. "I'll keep you updated, but for now, the sheriff's done with Ellen. You're digging into this, aren't you?"

Rebecca didn't necessarily approve of the investigations Moose and I had conducted in the past, but I wasn't about to lie to her. "As a matter of fact, we've already started digging," I said.

"Good. Find out who did this, the quicker the better," Rebecca said.

"Why so enthusiastic?" I asked.

"This is going to haunt Ellen and her kids until Gordon's killer is found," she said. "If it takes too long, she'll be branded as a murderer no matter what the outcome."

"We're going to do our best," I said.

"I'm sure you are. Well, I'll let you go. I just wanted to catch you up to speed about where things stood."

"Thanks for the call. I'm sure we'll be chatting again soon."

"You can count on it," Rebecca said.

"What did she have to say?" Greg asked as I walked back into the kitchen.

"Ellen's free, at least for now," I explained as I took a bite of the apple pie Greg had put out on the counter. "Was that for me?"

"Sure, why not?" he said with a grin as he got a piece for himself. "Have you and Moose had any luck so far?"

"We're just getting started," I said after I took another bite. "You know how it goes. We do the best we can, but we don't have a lot of control of the investigation. All we can do is keep digging and hope that something turns up."

"You'll find a way," Greg said. "I have faith in you both."

"Not misplaced, I hope," I answered with a smile.

"Never," he replied, matching my grin with one of his own.

"Ellen, I'm surprised to see you came in today," I said at the door of the diner the next morning.

"Why wouldn't I come to work?" she said. "I can't sit around the house all day waiting for the kids to get out of school. I'd go stir-crazy."

"I understand that, but maybe this isn't the best idea. You know how people talk in town. Are you sure that you're up to it?"

"Please don't make me go," Ellen said, her voice pleading. "I need this."

I put on my brightest smile. "Don't get me wrong. I'm happy to have you, if you're sure. Just promise me one thing. If things get too rough for you, you'll take off. Is that a deal?"

"It is," she said. "Thanks, Victoria."

"I should be thanking you for showing up. Martha's coming in later with Moose to take my place, and I know that you two get along great."

"Martha's a peach," she said as she tied her apron on. "I'm guessing that you and Moose are going to keep digging into Gordon's murder, aren't you?"

"You don't mind, do you?"

"Mind? I'd pay you if I could afford it. I don't have a great deal of faith in Sheriff Croft. He seems to be focusing all of his attention on me."

"Don't sell him short," I said. "He's a good cop. I'm sure that once he convinces himself that you didn't have anything to do with what happened to your ex-husband, he'll go after the real killer."

"I hope you're right, but in the meantime, I'm glad that

you and Moose are looking into it. Do you have any leads so far?"

I looked around at the two tables with customers, and I lowered my voice. "Do you really want me to get into that here and now? You're just going to have to trust Moose and me to do our best."

"I do, believe me, I do. I just thought I might be able to help."

"We'll take all of the help we can get," I said. "Do you have any ideas about who might have wanted to hurt him?"

"You need to talk to Sam Jackson," she said. "He's hated Gordon for years."

"What exactly happened between them?"

"All I know is that there was a business deal that went bad."

"What kind of business were they in together?" I asked.

"They were selling marijuana, and evidently Gordon left town with Sam's share of their profits. I didn't approve of it, and Gordon swore to me that he stopped, but I found out later that he'd been lying to me. Sam was furious when he found out that Gordon had run off, and I was afraid for my life until I convinced him that I hadn't known anything about it."

"We've got Sam on our list, but we didn't have any luck tracking him down yesterday," I said. "Moose and I are going to try again today. Is there anybody else we should talk to?"

"No, no one that I can think of."

"How about Mitchell Cobb?" I asked.

"Mitchell? Why would he want to kill Gordon?" She looked honestly surprised by the mere thought that her former classmate could be involved.

"I understand Gordon stole you from Mitchell in the first place," I explained.

Ellen shook her head. "Is that what he told you? Nobody stole me from anyone else. Sure, Mitchell asked me to the prom, but he understood when I told him that I decided to go with Gordon instead. It was stupid of me to do it, and I always felt bad about ditching him like that, but it's not like we were ever a thing, you know?"

"He never asked you out after Gordon left town for good?" I asked.

Ellen smiled softly. "Oh, he asked me half a dozen times, but I always said no. It wasn't anything against Mitchell. I just wasn't interested in dating anyone for a long time after Gordon broke my heart."

"Until Wayne asked you, right?"

"Wayne is a dear man," she said softly. "The kids absolutely love him."

"And how about you?"

She reddened a little. "I'd better clear that table."

"You didn't answer my question," I said.

"How about that?" Ellen asked, but that was all that she would say.

I had a hunch that Wayne had indeed found his way into her heart, and I hoped that Gordon's murder hadn't killed the romance before it had a chance to bloom. Ellen had been through a lot, and she deserved a little happiness in her life. As long as neither one of them had killed Gordon, they both had *my* blessing, for what it was worth.

Ten minutes later, I looked up from the cash register to see Jessie Blackwell walk into the diner. I was surprised to see her after the confrontation Moose and I had with her the day before at The Harbor Inn.

Putting on my best smile, I said, "Sit anywhere you'd like."

"Actually, I came by to talk to you," Jessie said a little uncertainly. "Do you have a second?" She glanced around and saw that Ellen was waiting tables. "And if we could speak outside, I'd greatly appreciate it."

I wasn't sure how much latitude I was going to give the woman, but then again, if she decided to hole up at the inn, I might never get the opportunity to speak with her again while she was still in town. "That would be fine. Give me one second, and I'll meet you on the bench out front."

"Thank you so much," she said, the relief obvious on her face.

"Ellen, can you cover the register for a few minutes?"

"What is *she* doing here?" Ellen asked me.

"She wants to talk, and I can't afford not to hear what she has to say. You want us to find out who killed Gordon, don't you?"

"Of course I do."

"Then I need to do this. Are you going to be okay?"

"I'll be fine," she said as she nodded.

"Good," I said as I squeezed her hand. "I shouldn't be long."

"If it helps me and the people I love get out from under this mess, take all the time that you need."

I walked out and found Jessie pacing up and down in front of the bench. She obviously had something on her mind. "What can I do for you?" I asked.

It startled her, and I doubted that the woman had even noticed me coming out of the diner. "First of all, I owe you an apology. I snapped a little when you showed up on the path yesterday. I was trying to wrap my head around the fact that Gordon was really gone, and then there you and your grandfather were, confronting me out of the blue.

"Jessie, how did you and Gordon get along?" I asked gently.

"We were engaged to be married," she said, the words rushing out of her in a well-rehearsed tone of voice.

"You didn't answer my question."

"Gordon was an interesting man," she said after a moment's reflection. "We didn't always see eye-to-eye, but I genuinely cared for him."

"Can you say the same about his feelings for you?"

It was a dangerous thing for me to say, but I wanted to see how she'd react. That might tell me more than the answer to any question I could ask.

Instead of blowing up, she just shrugged. "Now you sound

like my father. He never trusted Gordon's motives. In fact, Daddy insisted that Gordon sign a prenup."

"And did he?"

"He hadn't yet, but he promised to do it once we got back," she said.

I didn't put any stock in the dead man's promise. Gordon had evidently given up on the battle, but he hadn't conceded the war, as far as I was concerned. "Are you and your father close?" I asked.

"Not that much since Gordon came into my life, but we still talk once a week. As a matter of fact, I was speaking with him not a minute before you and Moose showed up on the path."

It was time to probe a little deeper. "We didn't mean to, but Moose and I overheard part of that conversation."

That earned me a sharp look from her. "What exactly did you overhear?"

"You said something about not thinking that he was bluffing, and that someone promised to bury you. Were you talking about Gordon?"

"I'd rather not explain," she said. "You're taking it all out of context."

"Then give me a little background," I said. "We'll do our best to help you."

"Why would you say that you'd do that?" she asked. "It's common knowledge how you feel about your waitress."

"We *all* want to find out who killed Gordon, don't we?"

"Of course we do," she said dismissively. "I got the impression yesterday that you wouldn't be all that upset if I'd been the one who killed him, though."

"That's not true," I said, stretching the truth a little. "While it's true that Ellen's a part of our family, we just want to know the truth."

Jessie shook her head. "The truth isn't always that easy to uncover, is it?"

"Well, all we can do is keep digging until we find it," I said. From Jessie's demeanor, and the words she'd used, I decided to play a hunch. "Jessie, were you afraid of him?"

She looked as though I'd caught her for a split second, but then she quickly composed herself again. "Nonsense. We were engaged to be married. I cared very deeply for him."

Why didn't I believe her? "Do you have any idea who might want to see harm come to Gordon?" I asked.

"I believe the police have a list of suspects long enough to satisfy anyone," she said. Again, it was a strict avoidance of answering my direct question. Had this woman been an attorney in another life, or did she always play things cagey?

"But do you know anyone who might have done it?"

"No," she said, one of the few direct answers I'd gotten out of her.

It was time to try a different line of questioning. "How long are you staying in town?"

"The sheriff has asked me to stay a few more days, and I've decided to indulge him. Daddy has offered me his lawyers, but I told him I'd be fine on my own."

I didn't doubt that for one moment. I was certain that the woman could handle herself in any interrogation, if the way she acted with me was any indication. There was no need to shield her from the police.

"Now, if you'll excuse me, I have several places still to visit," she said.

I couldn't just let her get away. I hadn't even had a chance to ask her about her alibi yet, but there was clearly not going to be time to do that now. "May we visit you at The Harbor later? I know that my grandfather would love to speak with you, and I'm sure that he'd be appreciative to hear your apology personally." It was the only ploy I could come up with to ensure that we had access to her again once we narrowed our line of questions for her.

"Of course," she said. "Just call first, would you? I *hate* to be caught off-guard."

"We will. I promise."

"Excellent." She glanced back into the diner, and then Jessie asked me, "Do you think I should say something to

Ellen? Things were said between us before Gordon died, and I now regret getting involved in their domestic issues."

"I'm not sure how receptive she would be to an apology just now," I said honestly. I didn't want to put Ellen through anything she didn't have to endure while so much was going on. "Don't get me wrong. She has a good heart, but this has all thrown her for a real loop."

"I understand how she feels," Jessie said. "Would you mind conveying my apologies to her directly, then? She might be a little more receptive hearing it from you. Please?"

"I'll tell her," I said, not at all sure how it would go over with Ellen. Still, it was the least I could do. I believed that Jessie was sincere about at least that much, and that she regretted the trouble she and Gordon had caused Ellen since they'd come to town.

"That's all that I can ask," Jessie said, and then she walked away.

I went back into the diner, took a deep breath, and decided that the longer I put it off, the worse it was going to be.

I needed to convey Jessie's message, no matter how unpleasant Ellen's reaction might be.

As I walked inside, I looked back over my shoulder. Jessie was heading toward a nice car, but that wasn't what caught my eye.

Wayne, my favorite mechanic and Ellen's current boyfriend, sat up in the car he was driving after she passed him, and as soon as Jessie pulled out of the parking lot, he was right behind her.

What was the man up to?

I didn't know, but I was going to make it a point to find out the next time I had a chance to talk to him. That was all we needed, more people trying to solve Gordon's murder and getting in our way. Moose and I had it covered, and at least we had some experience investigating.

All Wayne would do was mess things up.

Chapter 8

"Is she gone?" Ellen asked me as I walked back into the diner.

"She just left," I said. "Do you have a second?"

Ellen surveyed the tables, checked the order window, and then nodded. "We're in the middle of a lull. What did she have to say?"

"Among other things, she wanted to apologize to you," I said.

Ellen's gaze flared, and her face flushed a little. "What happened? Was she too afraid to face me herself? Why did she send you to apologize to me?"

"She asked me if she should speak with you directly, but I wasn't sure that it was all that good an idea. I offered to tell you myself, and if that was the wrong decision, you shouldn't hold it against her."

"Are you actually on *her* side, Victoria?" Ellen asked loudly enough to get the attention of our diners. Great. I'd been trying to avoid a scene, and now I was the direct cause of one.

"Lower your voice," I said, and she nodded. "You shouldn't even have to ask me that question. I was thinking of you when I volunteered to convey her message, but if I was wrong, I'm sure she'll talk directly to you about it. I was just trying to help."

Ellen nodded. "I know you were. I'm sorry I snapped. I can't help myself. When I think about Gordon trying to take my children away from me, with that woman's deep pockets behind him, it makes me so furious I could scream."

"You're going to want to fight that impulse," I said, trying my best to smile gently. "We don't need any help painting you with the 'Angry Ex' brush. Half the town probably thinks that if you did do it, you were defending your children, and I'm fairly sure none of them blame you for what happened to Gordon."

Ellen looked around the room, and a half dozen folks looked straight down into their plates. "Do you honestly think that many people in town believe that I'm a murderer?"

"I misspoke," I said, realizing how damaging that must have sounded to Ellen. "I'm sure most of them believe in your innocence."

"But not all of them," Ellen said. "Not by a long shot. I've lived in Jasper Fork my entire life. How could anyone think I was capable of murder?"

"Don't forget that plenty of them have believed it of me in the past," I said, "so don't feel like they're picking on you. Ellen, it's one of the reasons that Moose and I are searching for Gordon's killer. The longer it takes for an arrest to be made, the worse it's going to get for you and your family. Trust me on this one, there are more consequences from being convicted in the court of popular opinion than any trial."

"I know you've been in the center of these things before," Ellen said. "I thought I understood how you felt, but that was foolish of me. Until I started feeling the scorn of folks I thought were my friends, I had no idea how crushing the weight can be."

It was bad timing, but Margie Brewer chose that moment to pay her bill. As she handed Ellen a ten for a five-dollar tab, she said, "Keep the change, and hang in there. Even if this thing goes to trial, you just need one mother on the jury to keep your freedom."

"I didn't kill him, Mrs. Brewer," Ellen said.

"Of course you didn't, sweetie," Margie said as she patted Ellen's hand, and then she walked out of The Charming Moose whistling.

"She just called me a cold-blooded killer, didn't she?" Ellen asked me.

"Not exactly," I said.

"It was close enough, and you know it. You and Moose need to figure this out, Victoria, and I mean fast."

"We're doing the best we can," I said. "Are you sure that you're all right?"

"I'd be lying if I said that I wasn't a little shaky," Ellen said, "but I'm not going anywhere. Folks need to see that I'm not hiding in some corner, afraid of what might happen to me."

"That's my girl," I said as I squeezed her shoulder. "We'll figure this out."

"I hope you're right," she said, and then Malcolm Mason waved his coffee cup in her direction, and she grabbed a full pot as she headed off in his direction.

As I watched Ellen flit among our customers, I knew that she was right. Moose and I had to find the killer, and we had to do it before the town decided collectively that Ellen had taken that pipe to her ex-husband. I knew that Margie Brewer had been trying to be supportive, but she'd just confirmed my worst fears. If enough folks in town believed that Ellen was a killer, there would be no changing their minds later, even after the real murderer was brought to justice.

"Is Ellen working today?" Sheriff Croft asked as he walked into the diner a little after ten. "I thought for sure she'd be home."

"She wanted to come in, and I didn't have the heart to turn her away," I said. "Is something wrong? You're not going to question her here, are you?"

"No, your friend Rebecca made it clear that I wasn't supposed to talk to her without supervision," the sheriff said with the hint of a smile. "That was smart, bringing her in on this."

"She's never let me down before," I said. "If you're not going to talk to her, why are you here, then? I know that you're not a big fan of the diner in general."

"Nonsense. I love your pancakes, and you know it."

"Still, you don't eat here very often," I said.

"That's because I know where that will lead. If I want to keep fitting into this uniform, I have to watch what I eat.

Every now and then, though, it's good to indulge."

"So that's all you want; pancakes."

"That's it," he said.

"Then have a seat, and I'll be right with you."

"Does that mean that you're not even going to let Ellen wait on me?" he asked.

"She can do whatever she wants, but I have a hunch you're going to end up in my section, no matter where you decide to sit."

"Understood," he said. "If it's all the same to you, I'll have a seat at the bar, then."

"Sounds good," I said as I followed him. When he sat down, I asked, "Would you like a menu?"

"Thanks, but I don't need one. I'll have a half stack of your mother's pancakes, and a side of bacon."

"Wow, you really *are* indulging," I said. "Would you like some coffee to go with that?"

"Sure, why not?"

I flipped a cup over on its saucer and filled it for him. As I walked into the kitchen, I found Ellen chatting with my mother. "Do I have a customer?"

"The sheriff is here," I said.

Ellen stiffened instantly. "Did he come here for me?"

"Relax. He says he just wants a half stack of Mom's pancakes."

"And why wouldn't he?" my mother asked as she poured some batter onto the grill. "He used to eat them all of the time back when he first became sheriff."

"I keep forgetting that you've been running this grill for a long time," I said. "Does it ever get old for you?"

"I don't imagine how it could. Every order's different, isn't it?" Mom said as she deftly flipped three pancakes with her spatula, each one making a perfect landing on the hot griddle. I'd tried to make pancakes once, and they'd been an unmitigated disaster. There was a great deal more art to flipping than I'd realized, and I'd decided to leave them to the experts after that.

"I don't know. There are at least a dozen diners who order the exact same thing every time they walk through the door. I personally couldn't eat the same thing every day of my life."

"I don't know. There's comfort in finding something you like," she said as she removed the finished pancakes, glanced at the order I'd put in line, and added three pieces of bacon to the plate fresh from the grill. "There you go."

"Thanks," I said.

"Would you like me to deliver that order?" Ellen asked, though it was clear that she had no interest whatsoever in dropping off this particular order.

"I've got it. Why don't you extend your break a little until he's gone?"

Ellen shook her head. "No thanks. No one's going to keep me back here, not even the police." With a firm step, she walked to the counter and grabbed the pancakes before I could get to them. "On second thought, I'll deliver these myself."

"You don't have to do that," I said.

"As a matter of fact, I do." She put on a brave face, and then Ellen walked through the kitchen door into the dining room.

"I'm going to follow her," I said.

"Victoria, don't interfere. She has to do this herself."

"Maybe so, but that doesn't mean that I can't keep an eye on her."

I walked through the kitchen, and I saw that though Ellen had dropped off the sheriff's order, she stayed close by him. They were talking about something, and I didn't like the fact that the sheriff had apparently disobeyed Rebecca's request.

"Is there something I can help you with?" I asked.

"No, it's fine," Ellen said. "We were just talking about the weather."

"Was that *all* you were discussing?"

"Honest, that was it," the sheriff said as he held his knife and fork up in the air.

"Okay, but I've got my eye on you," I said.

He actually laughed as he responded, "Victoria, I'd be disappointed in you if you didn't. Tell your mother the pancakes are spectacular, as usual."

"I will," I said. "Ellen, it looks like Karen is ready for her bill." Karen Morgan was our local clerk of court, and she had started eating regularly at the diner lately. Some folks were like that, turning from infrequent customers to steady ones for a while, and then tapering off again. I never knew if it was because of our cooking or something going on in their lives, and it wasn't exactly a question that I could come right out and ask them. For now, at least, she was getting to be something of a regular, and I knew that her time was limited during lunch hour, so it was important that we be prompt.

"I'm on it," Ellen said.

As she delivered the bill, I waved at her to ring Karen up so I could talk to the sheriff in somewhat kind of private. "Are you behaving yourself?"

"Mostly," the sheriff said. "You know that I pride myself on being a man of my word. I won't ever do anything I've agreed not to. You don't have to worry about me."

"I'm not questioning your ethics," I said. "I'm just looking out for Ellen."

"Don't you think I know that?" The sheriff took another bite, and then he pushed his plate away, though there was still a fair amount of pancakes there. "That's it for me. I'd better quit while I can."

"Would you like me to wrap what's left up for later?" I asked.

"Don't tempt me," he said as he slid a ten under his plate. "I've got to be going. Thank your mother for me."

"I will," I said. "Sheriff, thank you for taking it easy on Ellen."

"Don't mistake my actions for leniency," Sheriff Croft said as he stood. "Ellen doesn't have an alibi for the murder of her ex-husband, and everyone knows that she had reason enough to wish him harm. She's by no means off my list."

"You're not going to arrest her, are you?" I asked. I

couldn't imagine Ellen ever getting over being handcuffed and led away from The Charming Moose Diner by the police.

"Not until I have a lot more evidence than I do at the moment. How's *your* investigation going?"

"What makes you think that *I'm* doing anything?" I asked.

"You and Moose would have to be locked up in one of my cells not to dig into Gordon's murder. Just be careful. We don't know who did it, but one thing is certain. The man didn't kill himself with that pipe. There's someone dangerous on the loose, and I mean to find them and lock them up, no matter who it turns out to be."

"I understand," I said. "Just don't be surprised when we give you someone else's name as the killer, and not Ellen's."

"Don't get yourself killed," the sheriff said with a smile. "I don't want to deal with the paperwork that would bring."

"We'll do our best," I said.

Ten minutes later, Mitchell Cobb came into the diner. We were getting quite a crowd for a time that was nearly too late for breakfast, but still too early for lunch. I wasn't about to turn anyone away, though. Our bottom line could use every customer who came through the door.

"Sit where you'd like," I told him.

Mitchell nodded in my direction, but instead of finding a table, he walked straight over to Ellen. I wanted to follow him so I could eavesdrop, but unfortunately, at that instant, half a dozen customers all decided at the same moment that it would be a good time to settle up their bills.

By the time I finished ringing everyone up and making change, Mitchell was on his way out the door, too, a scowl plastered to his face.

"Is something wrong?" I asked him as he brushed past me.

"Nothing you can do anything about," he lashed out at me just before he escaped.

I glanced over at Ellen, who was visibly shaken by something.

"What just happened?"

"Mitchell told me that he loved me," Ellen said, her voice shaking a little as she relayed the information to me.

"That can't really come as a big surprise," I said. "He's had a crush on you forever."

"It's not just that. He said that after what happened, I owed him."

"What did he mean by that?"

"I'm not sure, but I don't like it. I told him that I was with Wayne now, and that he was too late saying things like that. A few years ago I might have gone out with him, but I've got someone important in my life now."

"How did he take it?"

"You saw him. He nearly ran you over trying to get out of here," Ellen said. "You know what? Maybe coming in wasn't such a good idea after all. I hate to do it to you, but is there any way that you can cover for me for the rest of my shift?"

It wasn't even eleven yet, and Ellen was due to work three more hours. We'd handled things the day before, but I hated to put that kind of burden squarely on Martha's shoulders. "Let me call Jenny and see if she can come in early."

"I hate to ask her to do that," Ellen said.

"That's okay, you're not asking her anything; I am. What's the worst that can happen? All she can say is no."

"I appreciate you asking her," Ellen said. "If she can't make it in, don't worry about it. I'll find a way to deal with it. I won't let you down, Victoria."

"Let's just see what she says first," I said.

Jenny usually worked from four to seven every evening. I knew that she had classes in the morning before work and an active social life afterwards, but if we got lucky, maybe she'd have some time to lend us a hand. "Hey, Jenny, it's Victoria."

"I was just going to call you," Jenny said, and I felt my heart sink. Was she going to call in sick? I didn't know what we'd do without both of our servers.

"Is something wrong?"

"No, but I've got an offer for you. I know that Ellen's going through a rough patch right now, and I doubt she's all that crazy about coming in and working her shifts. My class schedule is fairly slow right now, and I can get some notes from my friends on what I miss, so if you'd like me to work double shifts for the rest of the week, I can make that happen."

"You are a lifesaver," I said. "Are you sure?"

"To be honest with you, I could use the extra money. Tuition keeps going up, and I could always stand a few more dollars in my checking account. Can Ellen afford to give up her shifts?"

"I have a hunch that right now money is the least of her problems," I said. "If you're sure you don't mind, that would be fantastic."

"Hey, it's a win/win. I can be there in ten minutes, if you need the help today."

"That would be tremendous. I'll let her know."

"Go on and send her home. I'm on my way."

I hung up and told Ellen what Jenny had said. "She's worried that she's taking money out of your pocket," I said. "Can you *afford* to take some time off?"

"Mom and Dad have already offered to help me with my bills this month," Ellen said. "The only silver lining in this whole thing is that it's clear that they're both really on my side. I think they blamed me a little when I married Gordon on such short notice, and then the kids came along so fast, there was a rift between us that's just now starting to go away."

"Well, it's good to be able to count on them," I said. "You can go ahead and take off. Jenny will be here soon."

"I have to wait on Mom, anyway. Her car is in Wayne's shop, so she's got mine. I'll give her a call to come pick me up."

"You can wait in back until she gets here, if you'd like."

"Thanks, but I might as well work while I'm here," she said.

I was relieved that Jenny was coming in to lend a hand. I hated the idea of leaving Martha at the diner to handle things on her own while Moose and I were off investigating murder, but with a full complement of servers, it wasn't an issue. I didn't know whether Jenny really needed the money or not, since I knew that her parents were helping her finance her education. She had a good heart, though, so her offer didn't surprise me in the least. We had been lucky with our hires at The Charming Moose, and I couldn't imagine running the place without either one of our current servers. Moose claimed that the diner always attracted the right people precisely when the place needed them, and I didn't have any evidence to the contrary to prove him wrong. I didn't want to have to deal with replacing either one of my friends, though if our luck held, I wouldn't have to anytime soon. I knew that someday Ellen would probably get married, and Jenny would graduate from college. That would mean finding a new crew, but at least I didn't have to do it today, or even think about it.

Our family at The Charming Moose was intact, and I meant to keep it that way if it was in my power. Now all I needed was my grandfather to get there with his wife so we could start investigating Gordon Murphy's murder again.

Chapter 9

"Where's my daughter?" Opal asked a few minutes later as she rushed into the diner. "Has she already left?"

"It's okay, Opal. She's in back with my mother," I said.

"What's Jenny doing here?" Opal asked as she pointed toward our other waitress with a look of concern. "You didn't fire my daughter, did you? *None* of this was her fault. It's not fair, I tell you."

"Hang on a second. First of all, would you please lower your voice?" I asked. "Ellen is in back taking a break. Nobody's getting fired. Why would you even think that I'd do something like that?"

"I don't know. I'm beside myself with what's happened," Opal said, her voice near its breaking point. "I need to see Ellen."

"Opal, would you like some free advice, worth every penny that it's going to cost you? You're not going to do Ellen any good right now with the way you're behaving. You need to take a deep breath, have a cup of coffee, and compose yourself before you speak with her. Can I pour you a cup?"

Opal resisted the idea at first, but after a few seconds, she nodded as she slumped down into one of the booths. "You're right. I'm sorry. I'm beside myself. Victoria, would you join me?"

The diner was starting to fill up, but I knew that Jenny could handle things for a little while. I wanted to talk to Opal about what had happened to Gordon Murphy, and I wasn't about to get a better opportunity. "I'd be delighted." I went for a coffee pot, and as I passed by Jenny, I asked, "Would you cover things for a few minutes? I need to talk to Opal."

"Sure thing, Boss," Jenny said with a smile. "Man, there are some really good tippers this time of day, aren't there?"

"I hadn't noticed, but I'm glad that you're doing well," I said. "Thanks again for covering the extra shifts."

"Keep it coming, I say," she said, and then her smile dimmed a bit. "I'm not happy about what Ellen's going through; you know that, don't you?"

"Nobody's going to doubt your motives, Jenny," I said. "Good."

I poured a cup of coffee for Opal, and then I filled another up for myself. It felt good sitting down with her, but I wasn't exactly on break. I needed more information on Gordon, and I hoped that Opal had some for me.

"It's a shame about your former son-in-law, no matter how you might have felt about him," I said as I took a sip. Usually I drank sweet tea, but I had the occasional cup of coffee, too. Any way I could get my caffeine was okay with me. When my dad had experienced his episode, he'd given up all caffeinated beverages, but I didn't know how he did it. My father was a lot like my grandfather in that respect. He had a tough time passing up a good story. Whenever someone asked him if he wanted a soda or a sweet tea, he'd tell them that the last one he'd had was in Intensive Care. I honestly believed that was what kept the man from having another one since.

"Gordon was a weasel, plain and simple," Opal said as she took a long sip of coffee. "I warned Ellen about marrying him, but she wouldn't listen, and now look what's happened."

"You haven't changed your mind, have you?" I asked her.

"What do you mean?"

"Opal, please tell me that you don't think that your daughter had anything to do with what happened to Gordon," I said.

She looked shocked by the question. "Of course not. My Ellen would *never* do something like that." She took another sip of coffee, and then Opal looked steadily at me. "There *is* something on my mind, though. Have you spoken with Robert?"

"Your husband was in here the day Gordon was murdered," I said.

"That's not what I meant. Have you spoken with him since it happened?"

"Not very much, but then again, we haven't had the chance to really chat," I admitted. "Why, do you think that we should?"

Opal shook her head. "No, I'm sure that Robert is innocent. I'm sure of it!" Why wouldn't Opal make eye contact with me all of a sudden? Did she suspect that her husband may have had something to do with Gordon's murder? And if she did, was there cause to believe that it might be true? One thing was clear; Moose and I needed to speak to Robert and decide for ourselves.

I touched her hand lightly. "Opal, are you trying to convince *me* of that, or yourself?"

Opal frowned, took another sip, and then she said, "Sometimes it's like I don't even know the man anymore, you know?"

"I can't imagine that it's easy for you, given the way the two of you live apart."

Opal shook her head. "It was never my idea. Robert was committed to the plan once the Jefferson place went on the market. He told me that it would be a good investment property for our old age. I believed him, but three days after we took possession, he told me that he wanted to live there full time. I know folks in town talk about our living arrangement, but I couldn't change his mind."

"Hey, if it works for you, I don't think anyone else's opinion matters," I said.

"Would you live apart from Greg?" she asked earnestly.

I tried to imagine what it would be like not seeing my husband right before I fell asleep or the first thing in the morning when I opened my eyes. "I don't think it would work for us, but that's just our situation, not yours."

"Well, it's me, too," Opal said sadly. She took another sip, and I topped off her coffee cup. "I really shouldn't."

"You don't have to drink all of it," I said. "How are Ellen and the kids holding up?"

"The children are in some kind of shock, and Ellen's doing everything in her power to hold it all together for them. They begged her to let them go to school today, though I tried to talk them out of it, but Ellen thought it would be healthy for all of them to go about their business, and nobody would listen to me. Now that she's here, I'm sure that she's regretting it. I just hope the other children at school aren't too brutal to my grandchildren."

It had been my experience growing up that while there were a handful of kids who knew how to show real compassion, the vast majority of them hadn't mastered the skill yet. I wasn't about to say that to Opal, though. "Well, they'll be home soon, at any rate."

"They aren't going home," Opal said. "They're all going to stay with me until things settle down." It was pretty clear that she was quite pleased with the situation.

"Was that Ellen's idea?" I asked.

"No, you know as well as I do that my daughter is fiercely independent. She refused at first, but then the first reporter from Charlotte showed up on her doorstep. They can smell blood in the water, and when they're going after a story, they are relentless."

I wondered just how true that was, since no one had come by the diner looking for a story about Ellen and her ex-husband since the murder. Chances were good that it had just been a stringer trying to find something to write about, and once she'd been rebuffed, the story was dead. "Still, it's awfully sweet of you to take them in."

"What's a mother or a grandmother to do," Opal said. "My home is always open to them." She took another sip of coffee, and it was clearly starting to loosen her up. "And if the reporters weren't bad enough, the police have been positively relentless. Can you imagine? They even asked me for *my* alibi."

"What did you tell them?" I asked.

"How can anyone say for sure? I baked that day, saw to the children, had a picnic with my daughter and her children, ran some errands, and I probably did half a dozen other things that I don't remember now."

"This is one of those times when it pays to be as specific as you can be," I said.

Opal looked as though she were about to elaborate when Ellen came out of the kitchen. She looked surprised to see her mom chatting with me.

Ellen walked over quickly. "How long have you been here, Mother?"

"It's my fault she didn't come get you," I said. "I offered her a cup of coffee, and I joined her," I said quickly.

"That's nice of you, but we need to go," Ellen said firmly.

"I understand that," I said as Opal and I got up from the booth. "How are you doing, Ellen?"

"I'm better, now that I'm going home."

"With me, you mean," Opal said.

Ellen frowned, but then she nodded in agreement. "We'll stay there tonight, but we're going back home tomorrow. Okay?"

"Whatever you want to do is fine with me," Opal said, but I noticed that there was more than the hint of a smile on her lips as she said it. This woman was clearly enjoying her daughter and grandchildren, and I had to wonder how lonely she must be with her husband living across the street.

"Will we see you tomorrow?" I asked Ellen.

"It's doubtful," Opal said before her daughter could answer.

Ellen frowned. "Mother."

"What? Isn't it true?" Opal asked.

Ellen turned to me. "I'll let you know, Victoria. Jenny's offered to work both our shifts for the next few days, and if you don't mind, I might just take her up on it."

"I want you to do whatever makes you feel comfortable," I said.

"I doubt coming in to work or staying at my mother's

place will make much difference one way or the other. We'll see."

"That's fine," I said as Greg walked into the diner.

"Hey, Ellen. How are you holding up?" he asked as he hugged her.

"I'm leaving, if that's all right with you," she said.

Greg offered his smile. "I'm happy to say that I'm not in charge of anything but the grill and the kitchen. If you need any executive decisions made around here, the boss is standing right there."

"Don't worry; I've already approved it," I said.

"Then I'm all for it," Greg said. "Now, if you'll excuse me, I have a kitchen to run."

"I'll be back there to see you in a second," I told my husband, and we all watched him stroll back to his domain with supreme confidence.

"You're a lucky woman to have that man in your life, Victoria," Opal said after Greg was in the kitchen.

"Don't I know it," I said with a smile. "Ellen, call me if you need to talk. I'm there for you."

"Thank you for your kind offer, but she has me," Opal said.

Ellen shook her head slightly, and then she ignored the fact that her mother had just answered for her. "I appreciate that more than I can tell you."

Once they were gone, Jenny grabbed the coffee pot. "They're quite a pair, aren't they?" she asked.

"Opal might be a little overprotective of her daughter, but I'm sure that she means well."

"I don't know how Ellen even *breathes* when she's around her," Jenny said with a laugh.

"Isn't your mother just as attentive?" I asked.

"Not since kindergarten. Don't get me wrong. She's there if I need her, but I have to be the one who calls her for help. She learned a long time ago that I was a big girl, and I could take care of myself."

"Well, we're not all as strong as you are," I said with a

laugh. Jenny had an infectious spirit, and I loved being around her.

"You're kidding, right? Victoria, if there's a woman in all of Jasper Fork who's more self-assured than I am, it's got to be you. You're the very definition of an independent woman."

"It's nice of you to say so, but I have a pretty good support system in place here and at home. I'm not nearly as autonomous as you might think. In many ways, my family is what makes me stronger and more assured."

"Some make us stronger, some fight to hold us back," she said. "Enough philosophizing; I've got work to do. I don't know how you manage to work all day. I'm already pooped, and my real shift hasn't even started yet."

"You can do it," I said. "The key is to take some breaks throughout the day. I don't work from six in the morning until seven at night straight through. I have short breaks from eight to eleven, and then again from four to five. We can work something out for you, too, while you're working both shifts on the floor."

"Thanks, but I want to see how much I can manage in tips. If I start to wear out, I'll let you know."

"You do that. Just don't kill yourself."

"I'll try not to, but you're not the greatest example of moderation, even *with* your breaks."

"So then do as I say and not as I do," I answered with a smile.

"I'll give it my best shot," she said as Mom came out from the back after being relieved of her duty at the grill.

"Victoria, do you have a second?" she asked.

Jenny flipped a towel over her shoulder. "I'll take care of the bar."

"What's up, Mom?" I asked once Jenny was gone.

"To be honest with you, I'm worried about Ellen," she said.

"Did she say something to you when she was back in the kitchen waiting for Opal?"

"She said a great many things. I'm afraid that she might be a little paranoid."

"What do you mean?" I asked.

"Over the course of thirty minutes, she expressed concern that her mother, her father, and even her boyfriend might have been involved in Gordon Murphy's murder."

"Did she say anything specific?" I asked. Maybe Ellen had picked up on some things that Moose and I hadn't been able to uncover yet.

"You don't think that she's right, do you?" my mother asked.

"Moose and I are still trying to figure out who might have done it," I admitted. "Maybe Ellen's heard or seen something that incriminates someone close to her, only she doesn't realize it."

Mom bit her lower lip for a second before she spoke. "Why do I feel as though I'm telling tales out of school?"

"Look at it this way. Did Ellen swear you to secrecy?"

"No, of course not."

"Did she even ask you to keep your conversation private?" I asked.

"No, not at all."

"Then you should be able to tell me whatever she said with a clear conscience." I meant it, too, and I had a hunch that my mother knew it.

"Well, she said that Wayne and Robert were both so angry with Gordon that they were both seeing red, but it was Opal's reaction that disturbed her even more."

"What happened?" I asked, trying to imagine the woman that I'd just had coffee with as a cold-blooded killer.

"She said that her mother had something on her coat when they were all at the park together, and it looked as though it might be blood."

"What?" I asked a little too loudly. If I remembered correctly, Opal hadn't even been wearing a jacket when I'd seen her at the park with Ellen and her grandchildren. "Did Ellen tell the police about it?"

"No. Opal told her that it was red paint she picked up by accident sitting on a newly painted bench at the park."

I thought about the benches Moose and I had seen where we'd found Ellen, and some of them *had* been freshly painted. Was Opal's story the truth, or was she using it as a cover for something darker? "I wonder if I could get that coat to the police? Does she know where it is now?"

"Ellen thought about that, but since Opal claimed that she threw it out, there's nothing she could do about it. Besides, the garbage trucks have already run. It's gone."

"The police still might be able to recover it," I said as I reached for my telephone.

"You're not actually going to call them, are you?" Mom asked as she put a hand on my arm.

"Of course I am," I said. "Mom, this could be important."

"Now I feel guilty," my mother told me.

"Unless you're the one who took a pipe to the back of Gordon Murphy's head, you shouldn't feel guilty about anything," I said. "Thanks for the tip."

"I wish I could say that you're welcome," Mom said, "but I'm having second thoughts."

I didn't even get the chance to say good-bye to her as Sheriff Croft picked up his line.

"I have a hot tip for you," I said.

"What have you been digging up now?" the sheriff asked a little sharply.

"If you don't want it, I'll just keep it to myself," I said.

"Hang on. I'm sorry. I shouldn't have taken out my frustrations on you."

"What's going on?"

"I'm getting some heat about Gordon Murphy's murder," he admitted. "I should be thanking you for any help you can give me. What's up?"

"Opal Hightower claims that she got red paint on her coat the day that Gordon was murdered," I said.

"Where did you hear that?"

"Let's just say from a friend of a friend," I said.

"I'll try to get a search warrant," the sheriff said.

"There's no need. According to my source, she threw it away in the garbage at the park, and the truck's already run."

"My deputies are going to just love that. Who's your source? Did Ellen tell you?"

"No," I said, since strictly it was true, though the information had come to me originally because of her. "I still don't know why it matters." There was a question I was reluctant ask, but I couldn't be queasy about it now. "Sheriff, was there much blood at the crime scene?"

"Not that she could have gotten on her," he said. "Without going into too much detail, most of the bleeding Gordon did was after he was already lying on the ground."

"So it's a dead end," I said.

"Most likely, but that's not going to keep us from looking for it. Anything else you need to share?"

I hated to do it, but there was something else. "Have you seen Robert Hightower's knuckles?"

"You noticed that, did you?"

"He claims he hit a concrete wall," I said.

"That's what he told me, too."

"Do you believe him?" I asked.

"The jury is still out on that."

"Do you think you'll be able to track Opal's coat down?"

"Don't worry. If it's out there, we'll find it," the sheriff said. "Thanks for the tip."

"Will you tell me what happens?" I asked.

"I guess I owe you that much," the sheriff said. "Keep those clues and tips coming."

"We'll do what we can," I said.

After I hung up, I wondered what the police would find. Was Opal the victim of wet paint, or was it something more sinister? Were Robert Hightower's bruised knuckles really the result of him punching a concrete wall? And what about Wayne? Had he taken matters into his own hands and killed Ellen's ex-husband? If he didn't think he could beat the man in a fair fight, which was fairly obvious at this point, had he ambushed the man from an alley using a pipe to the back of his head? There were too many questions for my taste, and not nearly enough answers.

For now, though, I had customers to take care of, and work of my own to do. Running The Charming Moose was a full-time job, and adding a murder investigation to the mix was just about more than one person could handle.

But somehow I'd find a way to manage. I'd done it before, and I'd do it again.

Chapter 10

"May I help you?" I asked a massive man in scuffed work boots, torn faded blue jeans, and a flannel shirt that was barely being held together with thread. He held an old grocery bag in one hand, and a beat-up baseball cap in the other.

"Hang on a second," the man said as he reached back and got the door for someone else. I was expecting more of the same, and I wondered if there was a heavy construction project going on someplace near the diner. That could be good for business. These men and women worked hard, and they could pack away a great deal of food without showing any signs of slowing down. "I've got two more coming."

I smiled my brightest smile, and then he stepped aside and allowed two little girls, one around five and the other around six, to come inside. They were both dressed in princess outfits, and each sported a glittery tiara that completed the ensemble. "Sophie, why don't you take your sister to that table over there, and I'll be with you in a second."

"What's my name?" she asked him with a frown.

"Sorry," he said as his face reddened a little. "I meant to say Princess Sophia."

"That's fine, Daddy," Sophie said regally. "Come along, Princess Elizabeth." She took her sister's hand in hers, and then both girls turned back to their father. "Go on. Ask her."

"I will," he said. "Stop bossing me around, young lady."

"But you're our squire," Sophie protested. "You have to do as we say."

Her father pointed to the booth, and apparently Sophie realized that she'd pushed him just about all that she could for now.

"I have a favor to ask," he said to me.

"What would the princesses like?"

The man grinned. "Ever since their mom got sick, I've

been taking care of them."

"I'm so sorry," I replied. "How awful."

"I guess I shouldn't say that she's sick. That's not really the case at all. My wife has been ordered by her doctor to stay in bed until the new baby is born. It's another girl," he added with a grin.

"How do you feel about having another princess in the family?"

"Just as long as she's healthy, I couldn't be any happier. The thing is, these two rascals talked me into having a tea party. The problem is, I told them we could have it wherever they wanted, and the scamps picked this place." He handed me the bag. "I know that it's a lot of trouble, and if it's too much, they'll probably understand, but I was wondering if we could get lemonade instead of tea in those, and a few cookies, too. You might not believe it, but those two are a tough crowd to please."

"Don't worry about a thing. We'll make it work," I said.

He nodded. "Thanks. I wouldn't ask if it weren't important."

"There's no need to explain. I was a little girl once, too," I said.

I hurried back to the kitchen and pulled out the most charming little tea set I'd ever seen from the battered old bag.

"What's going on?" Greg asked.

"We're serving tea to a pair of princesses and their squire," I said as I got lemonade from the fridge. "Do we have any cookies on hand?"

"Sure, your mom made some yesterday. Is sugar okay?"

"Did she top them with anything?"

Greg grinned. "No, but I can whip up some icing in a heartbeat, and we've got those sprinkles left over in the drawer."

"Perfect," I said. I rinsed the cups and the teapot, filled the pot with lemonade, and then arranged it all on a tray. Greg was as good as his word, and as I started to walk out front with the lemonade and now brightly decorated cookies, he looked over my shoulder.

"*That's* the squire?" he asked.

"He might not be dressed like one, but he's one of the best fathers I've ever seen."

"And even if he's not, *I'm* not going to be the one to tell him."

I delivered the tray with a flourish, and as I placed an empty cup in front of each one of them, I addressed them formally by name.

"Shall I pour?" I asked.

"Please," Sophie said with a bright smile.

I added lemonade to each cup, and then put the tray of cookies in the middle of the table. "If there's anything else you need, please don't hesitate to ask."

I stepped away, and Jenny joined me off to one side. She was grinning almost as much as I was. "What is that all about?"

"It's a tea party," I said. "Only they're using lemonade."

"Of course they are," she said.

The father raised one pinky as he took a sip of tea from the tiny cup. The entire thing was nearly swallowed up in his hand, but he didn't even flinch.

I waited on a few other customers over the next ten minutes, and when I glanced over at the three of them, the father motioned to me by writing in the air, a clear sign that he was ready for the check.

"I'll be right back," I said as I collected the cups, saucers, and the teapot. There were a few cookies left, so I wrapped them up after I rinsed out the tea service and put everything back into the bag.

As I handed it all to the father, he frowned as he looked around for the check. "I must have missed it. Where's the bill?"

"I'm pleased to say that the archduke has already taken care of it," I said as I winked at him.

The girls looked wildly around the room for their benefactor. "Is he here? Where's the archduke? We'd love to meet him."

"I'm afraid that he was called away on the queen's business, but he sends you his regards."

"The archduke is a fine gentleman," Sophie said with a deep air of seriousness.

"Let's go, Ladies. The queen is expecting us," their father said.

Sophie grabbed her sister's arm on their way out, chattering excitedly. "I can't wait to tell Mommy that the archduke was here."

"She'll be amazed," Elizabeth said.

"Thanks," the father said as he held the door open for his daughters.

"I should be the one thanking you. It was the most fun that I've had all day," I said, and it was the complete and utter truth.

"You get all of the fun ones," Jenny said after they were gone.

"It's always the luck of the draw," I said. I glanced at my watch, and then I added, "Would you like to take a little time off before Moose and Martha get here?"

"I'm fine. It feels as though I'm getting my second wind," she said. "I might take you up on it later, though."

"We shouldn't be long," I said. "Just let me know."

"Who are you going to interrogate first?" Jenny asked.

"I'll have to discuss it with Moose before I can give you a good answer," I said. "Sometimes we have different ideas about that."

"Knowing the two of you, I'm amazed that you ever agree on anything." Jenny seemed to reconsider saying that, because she quickly added, "Sorry, Victoria. I just crossed that imaginary line again, didn't I?"

"I won't hold it against you this time," I said. "Just don't let Moose hear you say anything like that."

"I'm not worried about him in the least," Jenny said. "He's a charming old guy, isn't he?"

"He thinks you're pretty beguiling yourself," I said, "and

we both know it." Moose had an obvious soft spot in his heart for Jenny, and it was clear to anyone who was ever around the two of them at the same time.

"What can I say? We're kindred spirits," Jenny said. "You don't think Martha minds, do you?"

"As long as you aren't Judge Dixon, you should be fine." Judge Holly Dixon and Moose were close, and closer in age, and my grandmother wasn't the least bit pleased about their friendship, though Moose swore that she had no reason to be jealous.

Jenny was about to reply when Moose walked in with Martha right on his heels.

"Are we late?" Moose asked in that booming voice of his.

"No, you're right on time," I said. "Thanks for covering for me again, Martha."

"It's always my pleasure," she said. I knew that my grandmother enjoyed coming in and working the front occasionally for me so that Moose and I could investigate, but she'd gotten a little rusty over the years, and balancing out the register was always a challenge when Martha was working the front very long. "I hope you find whoever killed that man. He might not have been an angel, but he deserved better than he got."

"Moose and I will do our best," I said. "Do you need anything before we go?"

She hugged Jenny, and then my grandmother said, "No, I'm sure that between the two of us, we'll manage just fine, won't we, Jenny?"

"Well, it won't be boring," Jenny said with a smile.

"I would hope not," Moose said. "Are you finished standing around gabbing, Victoria? We've got work to do."

"I've been ready since six a.m.," I said with a smile. "What's your excuse?"

"I may not have been here most of the morning, but that doesn't mean that I haven't been busy. I have a solid lead about where we might find Sam Jackson."

"We're not going back to the bar again, are we?" The

place depressed me, and I'd just as soon skip it today on our search for suspects and clues.

"No, not unless this other lead is a dead end. But there's only way we're going to know that, isn't there? Let's go."

I kissed Martha's cheek, and then touched Jenny's shoulder lightly. "If you two get overwhelmed, don't hesitate to call me," I said.

"We'll be fine," Jenny said. "Happy hunting."

"Okay, then." I turned to Moose as I said, "You heard the woman. Let's get cracking."

"So, where are we going?" I asked Moose as we walked out to his truck.

"No place that you'd ever expect."

As my grandfather drove, I asked him, "Well, are you going to tell me what our destination is, or do I have to guess?"

"It turns out that Sam Jackson's a big baseball fan. The high school is playing a game today, and I heard that Jackson doesn't miss a home stand."

"We're really going to a baseball game?" I asked.

"We have to go wherever our suspects are," Moose said.

"Fine."

"What's wrong, Victoria? You used to love baseball."

"I *still* do. I just hate to mix our criminal cases with my pleasure."

"I understand that," Moose said, "but it's the only place I could confirm where he would be, so we can't really afford to pass it up, can we?"

"You're right. I'm just being silly."

"Don't worry. It won't be that bad."

I looked at my grandfather and smiled. "Will you still buy me a bag of peanuts like you used to?" It had been our tradition when I'd been a little girl that Moose had always treated me to a bag of nuts when we went to a game, something I still remembered fondly.

"You can have two, if you behave yourself," he replied

with a grin.

"Then we'd better stick to one if you're going to place those kinds of restrictions on me. Do you think Jackson could have killed Gordon?"

"As far as I'm concerned, he's one of our likeliest candidates. Think about it. Who would you rather it be, a man who's known to live on the dark side of the law, or Ellen? If not our waitress, though, then one of the folks closely connected to her."

"We can't choose our suspects based on how much we like them," I said.

"True, but think about how nice it will be if it turns out that Sam Jackson is the one who hit Gordon with that pipe."

"It won't be that nice for him," I said.

"That's *his* problem." My grandfather parked the truck in the baseball field parking lot, and after buying us box seats, we went in search of Sam.

"He's right there, behind home plate," Moose said as he pointed.

"Who's that with him?" I asked. There was a familiar face there, but not one that I expected to see associating with Sam Jackson again. "Is that Mitchell Cobb?"

"It is indeed," Moose said. He turned to a vendor and said, "Two bags of peanuts, please."

I offered to pay, but my grandfather said, "Put your wallet away. This is my treat."

"Thanks." I took the offered bag, opened it, and cracked a few peanut shells. The nuts inside were warm and salty, and a flood of memories poured in with that first bite. I hated tainting those images with this investigation, but Moose was right.

I just needed to get over it.

"Are they as good as you remember?" Moose asked me.

I smiled brightly at him. "Even better. I could use a soda, though. I forgot how salty these things were."

"*You* can buy those," he said with a smile.

"It's a deal."

After I got us drinks, Moose asked, "Now, are we going to talk to our suspects, or are we going to order hot dogs, too?"

"Hot dogs? I could go for some hot dogs," I said.

"Victoria, we're here for a reason, remember?"

"Okay, fine. You win."

We approached the seats near Sam and Mitchell, even though our tickets were for seats that were quite a bit away from them. No one was going to mind, since the stadium was nearly deserted.

"Fancy finding you two here," I said as Moose and I sat down directly behind them.

"I was just leaving," Mitchell said as he started to stand.

"Don't go on our account," Moose said.

"I have to get back to the office. I just wanted to see what this year's team looked like."

"What are their chances?" I asked.

"They've got potential," Mitchell said, and he started to go.

Moose patted his jacket as he winked at me. "Victoria, I must have left my wallet at the concession stand. I'll be right back."

I started to stand as well, but my grandfather shook his head and looked straight at Sam Jackson. I got it. We were dividing and conquering. He was going to handle Mitchell on his own, and I got Sam. Good enough. I was sure that I could handle him.

As I settled into my seat, I said, "Word around town is that you had the best motive of *any* suspect to want to see Gordon Murphy dead. Do you happen to have an alibi for the time of his murder?"

To my surprise, Jackson started to chuckle softly. "I've got to hand it to you, Victoria. You've skipped the whole subtle approach and gone straight to the heart of the matter."

"Do you have an answer for me?"

"I'd like to help you out, but I didn't kill Gordon."

"Why should I believe you?" I asked as the batter got a base hit and the meager crowd cheered.

"You might find this hard to believe, but it's not all that important to me that you do," Jackson said.

"I saw how angry you were when you found out that Gordon was back in town. Are you trying to tell me now that you didn't do anything about it?"

"Oh, no. I confronted him," Jackson admitted as he watched the next batter swing and miss, and I nearly choked on a peanut.

"You're actually admitting it?" I asked.

"Why shouldn't I? He paid me back, with interest, a few hours before someone killed him. As far as I was concerned, it was over. Sure, I was mad at the time, but he paid me enough to make me let bygones be bygones."

"Do you have any proof that's what really happened?" I asked him.

Sam reached into his pocket and pulled out a thick wad of bills. The only denomination I could see was a hundred, and the rest could have been all ones for all I knew, but it was an impressive show of money. "How's that for proof?"

"There's no evidence that you got that from Gordon, and even if you did, how do I know you didn't punish him anyway after he paid you off?"

"Victoria, I've got to say that you're really starting to annoy me," Jackson said as he put the money away.

"Well, we can't have that, can we?"

"Why are you so interested in who killed Gordon anyway?" he asked me. "I can't imagine that you were that big a fan of the man."

"Ellen's a part of my family," I said. "I take all threats to her seriously."

"So, are you telling me that you might have whacked old Gordon yourself to protect your family?" he asked with the hint of a smile.

"No, *I* don't work that way."

"And you're implying that I do?" he asked as he swung around in his seat.

"I'm not saying anything," I answered. I was suddenly

uncomfortable having Sam Jackson's full attention directed straight at me.

"You need to be a little more careful about how you act around me." There was a sudden intensity to his words that made me glad that we were in a public place with a hundred witnesses around us. Sam Jackson was not a man I wanted angry with me.

"There's no need to get angry. I'm just asking questions, remember?" I asked.

"That doesn't mean that I have to like them," he said. "Maybe you should do us both a favor and find another seat."

"I don't know. The view's pretty good from here, Sam."

He frowned for a moment, and then Jackson stood. "Fine. You can have it. I'm done with this conversation, Victoria. I think that it might be a good idea for you to mind your own business whenever it concerns me. You're not a cop, no matter how much you might enjoy trying to be a detective."

"I do more than try," I said, not breaking our eye contact. "In case you've forgotten, my grandfather and I have solved more than one murder in Jasper Fork."

"He's not here right now to save you, though, is he?" Jackson asked. He was definitely threatening me now, and I could almost taste the anger in his words.

"I'm sure that I can handle you just fine without him," I said, though I didn't entirely believe that myself.

"I wouldn't be so sure if I were you. If you keep snooping into my life, you might just get more than you bargained for."

"Are you really threatening me?" I asked, doing my best to smile at him, though I had to admit that he'd shaken me, and more than just a little. This was one seriously bad man, and I might have just pushed him too hard.

"We're just having an innocent conversation, remember?" Jackson asked as he stood and walked to another section of the stands.

That had been productive, if I counted angering one of our primary suspects to the point where he felt the need to threaten me. At least life was never boring. I'd have to watch my back a little more carefully until the case was solved, but I wouldn't let Sam Jackson, or anyone else, keep me from digging into Gordon Murphy's murder. There was too much at stake.

Moose walked back to our seats a few minutes later. "What happened to Sam?"

I pointed him out, and then I told my grandfather, "He didn't care for my company any longer, if you can imagine that."

"Funny, I can handle it without too much of a problem myself," he said with the hint of a smile. "Were you able to get anything out of him, or did you spend the entire time just ticking him off?"

"He told me that Gordon Murphy paid him off, and he even showed me a wad of bills to prove his point."

"My, my," Moose said.

"I don't put much credence in it," I said. "There's no way to prove that he got that money as a payoff from Gordon, and even if Jackson was telling the truth about that, how do we know he didn't kill Gordon after he gave him the money he owed him?"

"You didn't just come right out and ask the man that, did you?"

I shrugged. "I might have said something to that effect," I admitted.

"So, you tried to antagonize him into confessing, is that it?"

"I thought it might be worth a shot," I said.

"Was it? Victoria, even if he didn't kill Gordon Murphy, we can't forget that he's still a bad man mixed up in some things we don't want to deal with."

"Hey, all I did was stir the pot a little." It was time to change the subject. "How did things go with Mitchell?"

"Not as well as I'd hoped," Moose admitted.

"So, he didn't confess, either?"

"He wouldn't even tell me his alibi," my grandfather said.

"Did he threaten you, though?" I asked.

"No, he was almost apologetic as he raced out of the ball park."

"Then I win," I said. "Come on, Moose, if our suspects aren't offended by the way we're asking questions, then we aren't trying hard enough."

"I prefer to think of my technique as one involving finesse," he said.

I had to laugh at that one.

"What's so funny, Victoria?"

"Moose, I'm usually the one who uses subtle questions to get information from our suspects."

"I know. That's what has me so worried."

I looked at my grandfather and saw that he was clearly upset. I touched his shoulder as I said, "Come on. It's not *that* bad."

"You can't treat our suspects this way, and certainly not a man like Sam Jackson. What were you thinking, Victoria?"

"I don't know. There's just something about that man that rubs me the wrong way, and I'm afraid that I let it show," I admitted.

"Well, you'd better learn to curb your feelings, or at least hide them better," my grandfather answered.

"I'll see what I can do. In the meantime, both of those men are still viable suspects."

"Until we get alibis from them, I'd have to agree with that," Moose said.

"So, where does that leave us?"

He broke open a peanut, ate it, and then took a sip of his soda. "I don't have the taste for these that I once had," Moose said as he wadded up the bag of nuts. "As for what we should do next, I don't have a clue."

"If you don't mind then, I'd like to go back and talk to Wayne at the garage."

"Is there something you know that I don't?" Moose asked.

I had a hundred smart answers for that one, but I decided to let it slide. "Earlier today, Jessie Blackstone came by the diner to apologize for the way she behaved."

"That's good information for me to have," Moose said a little chidingly.

"I'm telling you right now," I said. "I'm sorry, but there just hasn't been time to bring you up to speed on everything that's been going on."

"It's fine," Moose said. "What does Jessie coming into The Charming Moose have to do with us talking to Wayne?"

"When Jessie left the diner, I happened to glance out the window, and I saw Wayne following her in his car. I have a hunch that our favorite mechanic is doing a little sleuthing on his own."

"And you want to tell him to stop?" Moose asked wryly.

"Why not?"

"We're not technically supposed to be investigating murder, either," he said.

"No, but we have to be better at it than Wayne. I'm afraid that he doesn't have the right set of skills, if you know what I mean."

"Maybe, maybe not," Moose said. "He's probably not going to take kindly to us warning him off the case, though."

"At the very least, we can find out what he discovered following Jessie around. Who knows, maybe he found something useful."

"So, you don't want him digging into Gordon's murder, but you don't mind getting information from his investigation. Am I the only one who sees a little bit of a discrepancy in that attitude?"

"I never claimed to be consistent," I said.

"I'm glad," Moose said. As we headed up the steps toward the parking lot, he added, "Next stop, the auto repair shop. I just hope Wayne's done with sleuthing for now so we can hear what he's found so far."

"If not, we'll track him down later, but it's worth a shot."

"Agreed," Moose said, and we took off toward the shop to ask another amateur sleuth what he'd been able to uncover, and then ask him to stop digging. Moose was right. It was a dangerous tightrope to walk, but that didn't mean that it wasn't worth attempting.

I hated to see anyone risking their lives trying to find a murderer, and if that was inconsistent with the way that Moose and I ran our own lives, I could live with that.

Chapter 11

"We're in luck," Moose said as he pulled into the parking lot. "There's Wayne's truck right there. How do you want to handle this? Are you going to come out and call *him* a murderer, too, or is that just something you saved for Sam Jackson?"

"I told you, I admit that I was wrong the way I handled him. Besides, I don't think Wayne did it."

"Why, just because he's following Jessie Blackstone around town? That doesn't mean that he's innocent of the murder."

"How could it not?" I asked.

"Here's something that you haven't considered. What if Wayne killed Gordon, and he's afraid that Jessie knows. Who knows? Maybe she saw something that she didn't connect to the murder right away, and he's waiting to see if she figures it out? If Wayne is the murderer, what's to keep him from killing her, too, to shut her up?"

"Wow, you really do have a dark mind sometimes, don't you?" I asked.

"Tell me that I'm wrong. I've always liked Wayne."

I thought about it for a minute, and then I said, "No, when I look at things that way, you could be right. We need to be careful when we talk to him."

Moose looked surprised by my admission. "Are you really considering my idea? Are you willing to change your mind that quickly?"

"Of course I am," I said. "I'm a big enough woman to admit that I might have been wrong."

"Wow, there was enough wiggle room in that statement to allow you full deniability that you ever said it," Moose said with a smile.

"Let's just go talk to Wayne, okay?" I asked with a smile.

"Yes, ma'am. I'm ready if you are," Moose said.

We got out of the truck and walked inside the shop. It wasn't going to be the most comfortable conversation that we'd ever had with a suspect, but then again, it was never easy asking someone about their capacity to commit murder. To add another layer of difficulty to it, we were going to ask Wayne for information about one of our other suspects, Jessie Blackstone. I was glad that my grandfather was with me. This could get tricky, but between the two of us, maybe we'd figure out a way to get the truth out of one of our suspects.

It would make for a nice change of pace if we were successful this time.

"Wayne, do you have a second?" I asked the mechanic as we walked into his office.

"Sorry, but I'm trying to catch up on some of this paperwork," Wayne said as he fanned through the stack of papers on his desk.

"In a way, that's what this is about."

"How's that?" Wayne asked.

"We know why you're behind in your work," Moose said.

Wayne pushed back from his desk and stared at us in turn. He tried his best to smile, but it came out timid. "Hey, business is good. What can I say?"

"Well, it's hard to do your paperwork when you're out tailing suspects in Gordon Murphy's murder case," I said.

Wayne's gaze left us for a moment and returned to his desktop. "I don't know what you're talking about."

"You're not as good at tailing people as you might think," I said. "I saw you at the diner this morning. Did you learn anything particularly useful following Jessie Blackstone around town?"

"You really saw that?" he asked with disdain. "I thought I was being clever and crafty."

"I'm not saying that *she* knew that you were tailing her," I said, trying to save the man a little face. "But it was pretty obvious when she left the diner that you were following her."

"I've got a hunch that woman is up to something," Wayne said. "She's not the innocent lamb she wants people to believe that she is. You didn't see her at Ellen's the night before Gordon was murdered."

"What do you mean?" Moose asked.

"She was clearly uneasy around her fiancé," he said. "Jessie might have the big bank account, but it was clear who was running the show between them. If I didn't know any better, I'd say that she was afraid of Gordon. It's no great stretch to think that she might have killed him to protect herself, but you two haven't even considered her as one of your suspects, have you?"

"As a matter of fact," Moose said, "she's pretty high on our list right now. Why wouldn't she be? She was the closest person to him, and Gordon seemed to generate contempt wherever he went. We're not rank amateurs, you know."

"I didn't think you were giving her much credence as a suspect; that's all."

"Did you learn anything following her around town?" Moose asked.

"She didn't do anything all that suspicious at first, but then she met up with Cal Davies from The Harbor Inn. The reason I know him at all is because of the old junk cars he drives. I keep the man on the road most of the time, so I've gotten to know him pretty well over the years."

"It might not be all that significant after all. They know each other, so it's no surprise that they chatted," I said. "After all, that's where Gordon and Jessie were staying. Why wouldn't they talk?"

"You don't understand," Wayne said. "There was something odd going on there. She looked everywhere around when they met, and I thought for a second that they spotted me, but fortunately, I managed to duck back behind a tree at the last second, so they didn't catch me spying on them."

"Did you manage to overhear anything?" I asked him.

"A little. She handed him a fat envelope, and then she said

that was it. He wasn't going to get any more, so he should consider that his final payment."

That was indeed strange. "How did he react to that?"

"He laughed at her, but there wasn't a hint of joy in it, if you know what I mean. He said that he had one more coming, and that it wouldn't be over until he said that it was over. What's she paying him off for, anyway? What could Cal have on a woman like that?"

I didn't know, but I knew that we needed to find out. "So, the envelope was most likely stuffed with cash."

"I think that's exactly what it was. I deal with cash-only customers sometimes, and that envelope was a size and shape that I'm not likely to mistake. It was a payoff, plain and simple, and neither one of them wanted anyone at The Harbor to know about it."

"What are you going to do with the information?" Moose asked Wayne.

"What do you mean?"

"Are you planning on pursuing this?"

Wayne shook his head quickly. "No, I don't have the stomach for it. To be honest with you, I'm not cut out for this cloak-and-dagger stuff. I want to go back to running my shop; do you know what I mean?"

"We do," I said. "Digging into murder can be an awfully dangerous hobby."

Wayne sighed. "Well, I for one am done with it, so I'll happily leave it to you two." He paused, and then Wayne explained, "I just felt so helpless with Ellen, you know? I had to do *something* for her."

"Give her your love and support," I said. "That's the *best* thing that you can do for her."

"Yeah, you're probably right. Listen, I'd prefer it if you didn't tell anyone what I just told the two of you. I don't want anyone getting the wrong idea."

"Like the murderer?" Moose asked with a grin.

"Exactly. I didn't really think about it much before, but it turns out that you two are a lot braver than I am." He let out a deep breath of air, and then Wayne added, "Wow, I can't tell you what an incredible weight that is off my shoulders. From now on, I'm going to stick to what I know."

"Sometimes I think we should do the same thing," I said.

"No, don't do that," Wayne said. "You can't imagine how much faith Ellen has in your ability to track down Gordon's killer. She's counting on you two, not Sheriff Croft, to find out who the murderer is."

"We're doing our best," Moose said. "But we can't make any promises."

"Just keep trying. That's all that counts."

"Thanks, Wayne." I turned to my grandfather. "Are you ready to go?"

"In a second," he said. Moose flipped me the keys, and as I caught them, he said, "Go on out to the truck. I'll be right out."

I was clearly being dismissed, but I decided to give my grandfather some space. I walked out to the truck, briefly considered getting in the driver's side, but then I went to the passenger door and got in there.

Moose came out two minutes later, and I unlocked his door for him.

"What was that all about?" I asked him.

"I just told Wayne that there was no shame in stopping his investigation, and that Ellen needed him by her side instead of out on a case that might get him killed."

"Did you happen to tell him that he was still on our list of suspects, too?" I asked.

"There was really no need for me to do that," Moose said as he took the keys from me and started the truck. "He's acting as Ellen's protector, and I wanted to be sure that he didn't do anything else stupid."

"*We* do stupid things all of the time," I said with a grin.

"That's because we're seasoned investigators," Moose replied. I could see the twinkle in his eyes as he said it.

"But not trained ones," I answered.

"Our amateur instincts are what help us with the cases we

take on," he said.

"Do you honestly believe that?" I asked. I'd never really discussed our rationale for investigating murder cases with my grandfather much before, and it proved to be an enlightening conversation.

"I do," he said. "If the police's methods of investigation are what are called for, Sheriff Croft has a vast advantage over us. We can't run license plates, or use forensics, or implement the latest in police techniques. What we do have is a knowledge of the people in our area, and a general understanding of what drives ordinary people to murder."

"Well, that sounds about even to me," I said sarcastically.

"You're kidding, but I'm deadly serious. If it comes down to it, I'll bet on our instincts before I'll trust the police and all of the crime labs in the world."

"So, you don't believe the prevailing theory that we've just been lucky in the past?" I asked.

"Sometimes luck is when preparation meets opportunity," Moose said.

"Then what opportunity are we going to take advantage of now?"

"We're going to The Harbor. I want to have another chat with Cal."

"It sounds like a plan to me," I said. "What are we going to say once we get there?"

"Let's just wing it, shall we? After all, it's worked for us so far."

"It's a deal," I said.

However, all didn't go according to plan when we got to the hotel complex, no matter how unstructured our strategy might have been. One of my favorite expressions was that Man plans, and God laughs. This was no different.

As Moose started to pull into the only available parking spot near the inn, a security guard waved him off.

Moose rolled down his window and asked, "What seems to be the problem?"

"You can't park here, sir," the man said as he crossed his arms, pinning his clipboard to his chest. "It's for guests of the inn and the grounds only."

"How do you know I'm not either one?" Moose asked.

The guard tapped the clipboard. "I have your license number written down right here. Apparently, you've been here before."

"And that got my name on your list?" Moose asked. "I have a right to be here."

"While it's true that we can't keep you from visiting us entirely, we certainly have the privilege of telling you where you can park."

"Where would that be?" I asked.

The guard pointed to a break in the trees three hundred yards away. "Do you see that gap over there?"

Moose nodded.

"Well, you need to drive through that opening, and a little past that, you'll find a field where you can park another two hundred yards away."

"You've got to be kidding me," Moose said.

"Sorry. I've got strict orders." It was clear that he was enjoying ordering me and my grandfather around.

"What are you going to do if I park here anyway?" Moose asked him.

"Then we'll have to tow your truck," he said, and there was no mistaking his smile this time. He was clearly having the time of his life.

"Thanks. We'll move it," I said.

The guard seemed a little put off that we weren't going to put up more of a fight. He took a few steps back to see if we were indeed going to comply with his orders, and from his expression, it was clear that he was hoping that my grandfather was in a fighting mood.

"What do you want to do?" I asked Moose.

"I'm not letting that goon with a clipboard run me off," Moose said.

"But you're not parking here, are you?"

"Victoria, I have no desire to have my truck towed unless it's broken down by the side of the road. I'll park where he wants me to, this time."

"Okay. Let's go."

Moose backed all the way out of the spot and started driving toward the gap in the woods. As we turned the corner, he said, "You know, there's no reason for both of us to have to walk five football fields. Why don't you get out now, and I'll join you after I've parked?"

"I didn't think you liked us splitting up," I said.

"Come on. It's Cal. I don't think that you're going to be in any danger out here in the bright light of mid-afternoon. Find him if you can, but I'd appreciate it if you'd wait for me before you start grilling him."

"I'm not making any promises," I said as I got out of the truck.

Moose just laughed as he drove off. He knew that soliciting a promise from me had been futile, so I couldn't imagine that he was all that surprised when I refused.

I thought about going inside where it was air conditioned, but we'd found Cal outside before, and I had a hunch that was where he might be now.

I did my best to avoid the security guard, so I was walking a little stealthily around the corner when I heard a familiar voice coming just ahead.

It wasn't Cal, though.

It was Jessie.

"That's all you're getting, so don't ask again. I've reached my limit with you, Cal. If you insist on my paying you any more money, I'm just going to take my chances with the police."

"Do you really want to do that, ma'am?" Cal asked her. I peeked back around the corner and saw him tapping a fat envelope with his free hand. Wayne's story was panning out after all. Evidently, Cal was getting another payment, but Jessie had clearly reached her limit. He added, "I saw you hit your fiancé just before the man was murdered, and what's more, you drew blood."

"My nail caught his cheek. It wasn't a significant injury."

"Maybe not that time, but it proves that you have a fondness for violence, and I've got a hunch that no matter how hard you scrub your hands, there's going to be traces of Gordon's blood that won't come out. But even if you manage to clean your fingertips better than Lady Macbeth, you still left some evidence behind. I found your torn fingernail on the ground and I bagged it. The funny thing is, there's blood on the tip of it. Do you really want to take your chances with the police? I can be a pretty convincing witness, if it comes down to that."

"You're the lowest kind of worm. You know that, don't you?"

Cal didn't seem to take offense at her comment at all. He just smiled, and then he said, "I'd be careful about what I said, if I were you."

"You *know* that I didn't kill Gordon," Jessie said. "I was in my room when someone murdered him."

"Maybe you were, but you don't have any proof, do you?"

There was silence for a moment, so I looked back around the corner. Jessie was standing closer to Cal now, and the expression on her face had hardened somehow. "Don't push me," she said with cold inflection. "If I *am* the one who killed Gordon, you're playing a rather dangerous game with a killer."

"You don't scare me," ~~Gordon~~ Cal said, laughing.

"Then perhaps you should readjust your definition of the things that frighten you," she said.

"Jessie, you're looking at this the wrong way. I can be your best friend here, if you don't push me too hard."

"What are you talking about?" she asked.

"What would you say if I told you that I *know* that you were in your room the entire time?"

"How could you possibly know that, unless you were watching my room?" Jessie asked. It was clear that she was unhappy to find that Cal might have been spying on her. "As a matter of fact, I was checking on something for another guest, and I had a reason to linger in your hallway the entire time that Gordon could have been killed. With one more payment, I'll make sure the police believe me. Why shouldn't they? I'll actually be telling the truth this time."

"What are you doing?" Moose asked loudly beside me, nearly scaring me out of my shoes. I'd been so preoccupied with Cal and Jessie's conversation that I'd completely forgotten about my grandfather.

"Shhh," I said.

"Sorry," Moose said softly.

I peeked back around the corner, but both of them were gone now.

"What did I miss?" Moose asked me.

"Come on. We might as well head back to the truck."

"But I just got here," my grandfather protested.

"Sorry, but we're not going to get anything else out of Cal or Jessie right now. I'll tell you what I overheard on our walk back to the truck."

"We've got plenty of time to chat, then," Moose said in frustration. "It's more like a mile away than a few hundred yards."

I sincerely doubted that, but there was no reason to contest it. "I just caught Cal extorting one last payment out of Jessie. She told him that he wasn't getting any more cash, and he threatened her with going to the police."

"With what?" Moose asked. "Does he have actual evidence about the murder?"

"It surely doesn't sound as though he does. He did see Jessie and Gordon fighting soon before the man was murdered, though. She slapped him, and evidently she drew blood."

"How much do you want to bet he deserved it?" Moose asked.

"Whether he did or not is beside the point. Cal claimed that it showed that Jessie was violent with Gordon just before he died. I got something else interesting out of the conversation, too."

"What's that?" Moose asked as we continued our trek toward the tree line.

"Cal can alibi Jessie legitimately. He was doing something sneaky for another guest, and he happened to be in the hallway near Jessie's room the entire time during which Gordon was murdered. Can you believe he's extorting the woman with the truth? He can help her, but only if she continues to pay him."

"So, he tries to blackmail her with evidence of her fight with Gordon first, and when that plays out, he offers to alibi her. Why didn't he just lead with that, instead of backing her into a corner about the fight they had?"

"Think about it. If he could extort money without revealing any evidence of his own monkey business, the hotel would never have to know why he was lingering in that hallway."

"I've misjudged the man, and I'm not afraid to admit it," Moose said. "I thought he was back on the straight and narrow, but evidently he conned me, too."

"Don't feel too bad about it. The man is a slick operator."

"Maybe so, but I hate to be played."

"I understand that, but why don't we focus on what really matters? We can take two names off our list of suspects; Jessie and Cal."

"If Cal is really telling the truth," Moose said.

"He doesn't really have any choice in the matter, does he? Neither one of them could have possibly known that I was eavesdropping on their conversation. I believe that Cal was telling the truth when he said he could legitimately alibi Jessie for the time of the murder, and by doing that, he's alibied himself as well."

"Yes, you're right. That's what's most important, striking suspects and finding the real killer. It's still a pretty substantial list, isn't it?"

"There are more names on it than I like in the course of an

investigation," I admitted. We were just about to the break in the trees, and according to Moose, our journey wasn't even halfway over yet. "Shall we go over our list now, since we've got more time to kill while we walk?"

"Why not?" Moose asked. "Let's see. The folks closest to Ellen go on the list, so that's Opal, Robert, and Wayne."

"We can't forget Ellen herself," I reminded her.

"She didn't do it," Moose said emphatically.

"Show me the proof, and I'll do cartwheels in celebration," I said. "Until we have a reason to take her off our list, though, she's got to stay. If nothing else, it's only fair to the others we're suspicious of."

"I suppose you've got a point," Moose said.

"Then who do we have outside of Ellen and her circle?"

"I'd say that Sam Jackson and Mitchell Cobb have to go on it as well," Moose said.

"I understand Sam, but Mitchell? Is he really all that viable a suspect?"

"Think about it. He keeps popping up in our investigation on the outskirts. Is that a coincidence, or does he have a reason to be so visible?"

"I don't know. I always thought he was a quiet guy who kept to himself," I said.

"You've just described what neighbors say about serial killers after they discover what they've done," Moose said.

"Point taken. At least he doesn't use his middle name. That seems to be a real clincher, doesn't it?"

Moose thought about it, and then smiled. "You're right. I can think of three serial killers, and they all used their middle names. That's odd."

We were off the subject. "Can we change the topic of our conversation? Serial killers give me the creeps."

"I'm with you," Moose said. "Is there anybody that we're leaving out?"

I considered other possibilities, and then I said, "No, I think that just about covers it. If there was anyone else in town who wanted to see something bad happen to Gordon

Murphy, we haven't heard about them. I'd say that our list was large enough anyway, wouldn't you? I'm not afraid to admit that I'll be shattered if the real killer's identity comes from the top half of our list."

"Yes, it would be a great deal better if it turns out to be Sam or Mitchell. We can't count on that, though."

"I know, but I still don't have to like it," I said. "Hey, isn't that your truck?"

"It is, but the distance is a mere illusion. I must have walked half an hour coming to find you, and we've only been at it ten minutes."

"Time goes faster when you're having fun," I told my grandfather. "Besides, talking has helped pass the minutes, too."

As we got into the truck, Moose asked, "Do you have new ideas about how we should attack our investigation from here? To be honest with you, I was kind of hoping we'd be able to eliminate our friends before we started checking off the strangers involved in the case."

"I think we have to speak with the folks around Ellen a little more intently. She's probably still at Opal's or Robert's, and if she's not at either place, I'm willing to bet that she's with Wayne. There's something odd about her parents."

"What, the fact they live across the street from one another?"

"There's that, but each one has implied that I should look at the other as a possible killer. Doesn't that strike you as unusual?"

"They're both trying to protect their daughter," Moose said. "It's not all that strange at all."

"If you say so. That doesn't mean that we can let up on them, though."

"No, it surely doesn't. Let's go see if we can crash a family reunion and accuse them all of murder," my grandfather said with a wry smile.

"I'm not talking about doing anything that overt," I said. "We just need to keep questioning them."

"Agreed," Moose said. "Let's go see what the Hightowers have to say for themselves."

I pulled out my telephone and dialed the sheriff's number, but it went straight to voicemail. What I had to tell him wasn't something that I could leave in a message, so I told him to call me back when he could.

"Who did you just call?" Moose asked.

"I tried to phone the sheriff so I could tell him about Cal and Jessie, but he didn't pick up."

"He must have been doing important police business," Moose said with a smile.

"He's got his investigation, and we've got ours," I said. "I just wish that he'd be more forthcoming about *his* findings."

"Moose, we always knew that it wasn't going to be a two-way street. The sheriff has a completely different job description than we do."

"Victoria, are you actually taking up for the man?"

"No, but I can still acknowledge that he's got it a lot tougher than we do. We aren't restricted by any rules or regulations about the way we can look for evidence."

"We don't have a police force at our disposal, either," Moose said.

"Fair enough. I'm just saying, he's dropped a few hints to us in the past, and if we keep him updated on what we're up to, there's a better chance that he won't shut us down. Admit it. You'd hate to sit idly by while a murderer goes free."

"No more than you would," Moose said.

"I'm not disagreeing with you," I said. "I figure he'll try to get in touch with me later."

"Knowing the sheriff, I'm sure that you'll hear from him before nightfall."

"I hope that he's not at either of the Hightower residences," I said. "It's always awkward when we show up to interrogate someone that he's already talking to."

Chapter 12

"Are we interrupting anything?" I asked the Hightower family after they let us into Opal's place. To my surprise, Robert was there, as well as Ellen. We were in luck; there wasn't a police officer anywhere in sight when we showed up. "Where are the kids?"

"They're sleeping over at a friend's house," Ellen said. "I thought it might be a little too much to put them through all of this drama."

"You must miss them," I said. I knew how devoted Ellen was to her children.

"Every minute that we're apart, but this is for the best. Mom made me realize that."

Opal nodded as she laid her latest knitting project down on the table. "Children need stability in their lives. Can I get you something to eat?"

Moose and I had skipped lunch, and I could feel the hunger pangs beginning, but I didn't want to eat there, not with three of our suspects in the house. I was probably being paranoid, but what if one of them decided to get rid of us, too? A little poison mixed in with the food, and Moose and I would be finished with our investigation forever. I knew that the thought wasn't all that rational even as it popped into my head, but I still couldn't help myself. "Thanks, but we're eating soon ourselves. It's going to be really special, so we'd better not ruin our appetites."

Moose looked at me, questioning the statement with his gaze. I nodded slightly, and he joined right in with my lie. "Martha and Greg are preparing a feast for us tonight," he said heartily.

"Well, then," Robert said, "What can we do for you?"

"We were wondering if we could have a chat," I said.

He stood. "I'd be happy to, but I'll have to take a rain

check. I was just going across the street to have a smoke. I know it's a bad habit that's probably going to kill me someday, but I can't seem to help myself."

"I'll walk over with you," I said, making a snap decision.

"You don't smoke," Moose said to me.

Thanks for stating the obvious, I thought. "No, but I wouldn't mind stretching my legs a little. Come on, Robert. I'll keep you company."

"I don't want you to breathe any secondhand smoke on my account." Wow, Robert really didn't want me going with him. Was he afraid of what I might find out if he spent a little time alone with me?

"Nonsense. I insist."

"Very well," Robert said, but he clearly wasn't pleased by the prospect of having me for company.

We walked across the street to his place together, and he settled in on the porch with his back against one of the columns holding the roof up.

I found a spot upwind from him.

Robert lit a cigarette, and then he frowned at it. "I must have stopped a dozen times over the years, but I always come back to them, especially in times of stress."

"Are you under any undue pressure right now?" I asked.

"Do you mean besides the fact that my daughter's ex-husband was murdered, and everyone I love is a suspect? What do you think?" he asked as he took another puff. After a moment, he snuffed it out in an overflowing ashtray. "That's all that I'm allowing myself," he said. "It's not a perfect system, but I'm doing what I can to hold it together."

"How's Opal handling things?" I asked.

"I'm worried about her," Robert said.

"Is there any reason in particular?"

"She hasn't been herself since Gordon came back into town," Robert said. "I don't know what's going on with her."

"Do you suspect her of having something to do with what happened to your former son-in-law?"

He took a deep breath, and then let it out slowly. "I don't

know what to think anymore. Ellen loves her children, and if it were possible, I'd say that Opal loves them even more. What would either woman do to keep them safe?"

"I hate to think either would be capable of killing someone," I said.

"Well, you and I don't know the strength of the bond between a mother and her children, Victoria, no matter how much we speculate."

It was true that I wasn't anybody's mother, at least not yet, but I felt as though I could guess what it must be like. "We might not have children, but we've both been on the other side of that bond. I can say with all certainty that my mother wouldn't do it."

Almost as an unconscious act, Robert reached down, grabbed another cigarette from the pack, and then lit it. "Your mother is a strong woman. She wouldn't sit idly by while someone was threatening you, nor would your grandmother."

"Are you discounting my father and my grandfather?" I asked.

"No, the entire town knows how much those two men love you, but the bond between mother and child is extra special. When Ellen was growing up, I was fine to have fun with, but whenever things got serious, or when she was the slightest bit sick or injured, only her mother would do. To be honest with you, it kind of hurt my feelings at first, but I got used to it over time."

"So, you believe that both your wife *and* your daughter are capable of murder," I said.

He hesitated, took another drag from his cigarette, and then snuffed it out as well. "It sounds really harsh when you put it that way."

"That's what it boils down to, though, isn't it? It's cold-blooded murder to hit a man in the back of the head with a pipe when he can't defend himself."

Robert frowned and shook his head. "Perhaps, but then again, maybe it is the lesser of two evils." He stared off into

space, and then ran a hand through his hair. The act made
him wince a little, and I had to wonder if his bruised hand
wasn't still killing him. "I don't know what to think. Do you
believe for one second that I enjoy thinking of Ellen and Opal
as potential killers? Sometimes I wish that I'd done it for
them, so that they'd be spared Gordon's threats."

"Are you saying that you didn't kill him?" I asked. There
was nothing subtle about the question, but I was done
dancing around it.

"I didn't do it," he said flatly, though he wouldn't meet
my gaze as he said it. "I don't suppose that you have any
reason to believe me, but there it is."

"Let's say for argument's sake that you *are* innocent," I
said.

I was going to finish the thought when he interrupted me.
"Let's not. I'm many things, Victoria, but you can't list
innocent among them. I've done a great many things in my
time that I'm not proud of, but I've never killed anyone."

"Then who do you think really did?" I asked.

I could tell that he had a solid suspect, at least in his own
mind. It was clear by the way his eyes flashed and his lips
tightened, but all he said was, "It could have been anybody."

"You were going to say something else for a split second
there, weren't you?" I asked.

I honestly thought that he was about to answer, when Opal
came out onto her porch across the street. "Robert, we're
going to be eating soon. You're welcome to join us."

As he started to stand, Robert Hightower called out,
"Thank you. I'll be right there."

As we walked back across the street together, Opal asked
me, "I know that you have plans, but are you sure you don't
want to join us?"

"Thanks for the invitation, but Moose and I need to go."

My grandfather met me on the front porch, and we
thanked the Hightowers for speaking with us.

"We'll be in touch," I said as we left them.

Opal frowned, as though what she wanted most was for us

to leave her family alone, but Ellen smiled at us as she joined her mother on the porch.

"If it's okay with you, I'm coming into work tomorrow," she said.

"You don't have to," I said. "Jenny's glad to handle your shift."

"Tell her that she can sleep in, anyway. I'll trade off with her at eleven when Greg gets there. How's that for a compromise? I swear I'll be more focused tomorrow, and I won't let idle whispers distract me from my job."

"Who's been whispering about you behind your back?" Opal asked, clearly concerned by the thought of someone disturbing her daughter.

"It's not important, Mom," Ellen said with a smile, before she turned back to me. "My mother always did watch out for me."

"Don't forget your dad," Robert said with a smile.

"Okay, my dad, too. I'll see you in the morning, Victoria."

"I'll see you then," I said.

After my grandfather and I headed back to the truck, I said, "Before we go back to the diner, I'd like to go by the murder scene."

Moose nodded. "I'd be happy to, but what makes you think we'll get anything out of it that Sheriff Croft hasn't already discovered?"

"I don't know. Humor me, okay?"

"Okay," Moose said. "It's on the way back to the diner, anyway."

As he neared the alleyway where Gordon had been murdered, I said, "Pull over right here."

He did as I asked, and we both got out and moved to the sidewalk. As I looked up and down the street, I tried to imagine it the day of the murder. It was sometime around the same time of day, and the street wasn't very crowded at all. How did the shops manage to stay afloat? As we walked to the scene, I noticed that the yarn shop had a sign on the door

with its business hours. It was closed now, but it had been
open the day of the murder. It might be nice to talk to the
owner, but I didn't have a clue how to find her.

Moose and I walked a little into the alley, and I wondered
where Gordon Murphy had been standing when he'd been
struck down. Had he been facing the street, or the alley? That
could matter, based on where his killer had stood. There were
no windows along the way, just a few solid steel doors that
were all closed. Chances were good that no one had
witnessed the crime from there.

"It's kind of grim, isn't it?" Moose asked me in a soft
voice.

"It's always sad to visit a crime scene," I said, my voice
matching his. Why were we whispering? Out of respect?
Neither one of us had respected Gordon, but that didn't mean
that we couldn't lower our voices because he'd lost his life
where we stood.

As we walked out of the alley, we turned toward the
hardware store. On a whim, I walked in, but the owner
wasn't in his usual spot up front. I asked the young clerk, "Is
Jack around?"

"I think he's at the diner," he said with a grin. "You must
have just missed him."

"Thanks," I said, and Moose and I left.

"What was that all about?" my grandfather asked me.

"Let's go see if we can catch Jack, and I'll show you," I
said.

As my grandfather drove, I said, "It's probably a good
idea that we're headed back, anyway. I've got a hunch that
my servers could use a break."

"Don't worry about my wife. Martha can handle her end
of it," Moose said.

"Maybe so, but Jenny has to be beat. Not everyone can
work all day."

"Just you, maybe?" Moose asked with a grin.

"Not even me, not without a lot of breaks. By the way,

while I was with Robert, did you have any luck talking to Opal and Ellen?"

"That disappearing act of yours was brilliant," Moose said. "I didn't even think about the possibility of going across the street with Robert."

"That's why there are two of us," I said with a smile. "So, did you have any luck?"

"No, unfortunately, neither Ellen or Opal wanted to talk about Gordon Murphy. Not that I can blame them. The man came back into their lives to wreak havoc, and then someone stopped him from following through on his threats of taking Ellen's children away from her. It must have seemed like a dream come true to them."

"Do you honestly think they were pleased that someone murdered Gordon?"

"I doubt many tears were shed for the man," Moose said.

"Maybe not, but neither woman strikes me as being a cold-blooded killer. The funny thing was that Robert didn't seem to share your opinion of the women in his life."

Moose looked at me sharply. "Did he honestly say that he thought that one of them might have done it?"

"No, he didn't come out and accuse either one of them of murder, but he did imply that he could understand the urge if one of them decided to take matters into their own hands."

"Is there a chance that he was just trying to deflect your suspicions away from him?" Moose asked.

"I suppose it's possible, but it's kind of drastic throwing his wife and his daughter under the bus to save himself."

"People have done stranger things than that to keep from going to prison," my grandfather said.

"He made an interesting point while we were chatting," I said. "He claimed that the bond between a woman and her child is stronger than a father's bond with his kids."

"I don't know if it's always true, but I can see why he might think that," Moose said.

"Do you feel that way about Dad? Is Martha closer to him than you are?"

My grandfather frowned, and for a full minute, I wasn't sure that he was even going to answer my question, but he finally said, "She is, as much as I hate to admit it. I always tended to push your father a little harder than I probably should have. I expected great things from him."

"Is he really that big a disappointment to you?" I asked. I knew that there was an underlying tension between my grandfather and my dad, but I'd never heard Moose state it so boldly.

"Of course not. I couldn't love him any more if he were my own son," Moose said automatically.

"You tell that joke a lot; you know that, don't you?"

"Do I?" Moose asked.

"You do, and to be honest with you, Dad flinches whenever he hears you say it."

Moose frowned, and after a moment's thought, he nodded. "Then I'll have to stop repeating it, won't I? Is there anything else I say that's hurtful?"

"Come on, I didn't mean it that way," I said.

"No, you were right to point it out to me. Thank you, Victoria. Do you realize that *you're* a point of contention between us, too?"

I looked at my grandfather oddly. "Me? What do I have to do with your relationship with your son?"

"You and I have a closeness that your father and I could never manage. How do you think he feels when he sees us getting along so grandly?" Moose asked.

"He knows that I love him, too," I said defiantly.

"No one doubts that," Moose said. "I shouldn't have said anything. It's not your fault. It's who you are."

"Wow, thanks for that," I said sarcastically. Did I really show more fondness for my grandfather than my own dad?

"I'm sorry. I shouldn't have said that. Forget it."

"I would if I could," I said as Moose pulled up in front of the diner.

I left him to park the truck. I had some thinking to do.

To my delight, my father was at the diner with my mother having a bite to eat. I walked straight to him, put my arms around him, and hugged him tightly. After our embrace, I pulled back a little so that I could look him straight in the eye. "You know how much I love you, don't you?"

He looked startled by the question, but he nodded and smiled. "Of course I do. I love you, too."

"Hey, how about me?" Mom asked.

I hugged her as well. "I love you both. Equally."

"That's always nice to hear, but what brought that on?" Mom asked.

"I just wanted to make sure you both knew how I felt," I said.

"Well, we do," Dad said.

Moose came back in, blew a kiss to his wife, and then headed straight to his son. To the surprise of everyone there, he hugged him just as I had. "I don't say it nearly enough, but I love you, Son, and I'm proud of the man that you've become."

Dad was thoroughly confused now. "Okay, am I dying or something? Is there something that you two aren't telling me?"

"We've just been dealing with a lot of family intrigue with Gordon Murphy's murder," I said. "It's made us both realize again how much our family means to us."

"Hey, where's my hug?" Greg asked from the kitchen. "It's not fair. I'm the one slaving away over a hot griddle, and yet no one is showing me any love."

"I'll correct that immediately, then," I said with a smile as I walked to the door between the kitchen and the dining room and hugged him as well.

"Excuse me," Jack Kiley said, "but if you're all through with your hugfest, I could use a refill on my sweet tea."

"So, you're not interested in a hug to go along with it?" Moose asked him with a smile.

"No offense, but not from you," Jack answered.

"None taken. I don't blame you a bit, but it appears that

we've used up our portion of hugs for today. You'll have to take a rain-check."

"That I'll do, but I'd still like the tea."

"Coming right up," Jenny said.

"I'll take care of it." I grabbed the pitcher of tea and refilled Jack's glass. "Don't go anywhere. I need to talk to you."

Jack looked at me and grinned. "Am I in trouble?"

"No, I just want to ask you a few questions. Give me a second, okay?"

"Okay," he said.

I walked over to Jenny and said, "You can take off, Jenny, if you'd like the rest of the night off."

Jenny smiled at me. "Don't worry about me. I'm fine."

"I'm sure that you are, but it's hard to do this job all day without more of a break than you're getting. Take advantage of my offer and go home. You can sleep in tomorrow, too. Ellen's going to work until eleven, if that's okay with you."

"Are you sure that she doesn't mind?"

"Just between us," I said in a quiet voice, "I think being with her parents around the clock might be driving her a little stir crazy."

"I can respect that," Jenny said. As she took her apron off, she said, "If you're sure you can handle things here, I gratefully accept. I'm not afraid to admit it. I really am beat. Victoria, I have a whole new respect for you after what I've been through today."

"We all play an important part in keeping The Charming Moose running smoothly," I said, "but thanks for the thought."

"See you tomorrow." She paused, and then Jenny added, "If Ellen changes her mind once she gets here, I'm just a telephone call away, okay?"

"Okay, and thanks again for stepping in, Jenny."

"It's been my pleasure. Your grandmother is fun to work with."

"She has her charms, doesn't she?"

"That's one way to put it," Jenny said. I saw her stop and say something to Martha on her way out, something that caused my grandmother to smile. Jenny was like that, spreading smiles wherever she went, and I knew yet again that we were lucky to have her.

"Well, we're taking off," Dad said as he and Mom approached. They were on their way out the door when my father pulled me aside. "Are you okay, kiddo?"

He hadn't called me that since I was child, with the exception of a few times when I'd been in some serious trouble.

That's how I knew that he was really worried about me.

"I'm great, Dad."

"What really brought on that hug?" he asked quite seriously.

"I don't always tell you how much you mean to me," I said. "I know that I spend a great deal of my free time with Moose, but that doesn't mean that I love you any less."

"Victoria, listen to me carefully. I've never resented the relationship you have with my father. Would I like the two of us to be closer? You know what? We're close enough. He loves me, and I love him, as hard as that is for me sometimes. You two are a great deal more similar to each other than either of you are to me."

"And you don't really have a problem with that? Be honest with me," I said.

"I'm just glad that you each found someone who could stand to be around the other one," he said with a big grin, and kissed the tip of my nose, another thing he hadn't done in ages. It made me feel like a little girl again, and I was glad again for who my father was. Moose and I were close, but a girl's father is not easily replaced.

Jack called me over, and as I approached, he said, "As much as I love eating here, I have to get back to work." He pushed the plate away and smiled. "That's the best lasagna I've ever had in my life. Who made it?"

"That's one of Greg's specialties," I said. "It's one of my

favorites, too, but honestly, he's so good, my list of favorites is a mile long."

"I understand completely. Now, what is this all about?"

I took the seat beside him and said, "This won't take a minute. Have the police spoken to you about the day of the murder?"

Jack frowned. "Sure, of course they did. They wanted to know if I'd seen anything suspicious that day. I told them no, and they went away."

"That's the only thing they asked you?" I asked.

"The deputy seemed to have something else on his mind," Jack said. "Besides, what else could he have asked me?"

"Do you sell pipe like the one that was used to kill Gordon?"

Jack just shrugged. "Sure, but it's not like I'm the only supplier. I sell a great many things at the hardware store in the course of a day."

"Any pipe that day, though?" I asked.

"No, I don't think so. One of the guys might have rung something up while I was helping someone else, but I don't believe anyone sold pipe."

That brought out a new thought. "Would you know every customer who came into the hardware store that morning and afternoon?"

"Yes," he said, and there was no room for debate.

"Really? You just said someone else might have sold some pipe while you were away from the register. How can you be so sure?"

"Because I might not make every sale, but I know who shops in my store," he said, and I didn't doubt it for one second. Jack prided himself on his personal touch with customers, and I'd experienced it myself on more than one occasion.

"Okay, good. Did any of these people come into the hardware store the day of the murder?" I named our complete suspect list, including Ellen.

Jack stretched his neck a little as though it helped him

think. "Robert was there getting some caulk, and Mitchell came by to have a key made. That's it."

"And you're certain neither bought any pipe?"

"Positive," he said.

"Let me ask you one more thing. Is there a chance that one of them stole it?"

That clearly didn't make Jack happy at all. "I lose some every month to theft, I know that, but we do what we can. I can't say for sure that no one took a length of pipe if he shoved it down his pants."

"Do you keep a good inventory of things like that?"

Jack shook his head. "Not good enough. Our numbers are a little sketchy on things like that. Sorry I couldn't help."

I smiled at him as I grabbed his check. "You helped me a great deal. Lunch is on the house."

"I wasn't looking for a free meal," Jack protested.

"That's why it's so much fun to give you one," I said.

"Victoria, the City's been using that alley to store some construction materials. They cleaned it up after the murder looking for clues, but that pipe shouldn't have been that hard to find. Whoever got it didn't have to take one step into my hardware store."

"Maybe not, but if it's all I've got, I'm going to use it. Thanks again."

"At least let me leave a tip," Jack said.

"I can't stop you," I said with a smile, and then I tore up his check.

Moose walked over after Jack left. "What was that all about?"

"You could have come over," I said.

"I didn't want to cramp your style. Did Jack help any?"

"He told me that Robert and Mitchell shopped in his store the day of the murder, that he couldn't account for every pipe he had in inventory, but most important of all, he said that the alley was full of construction materials at the time of the murder, so the murder weapon most likely came from there."

"It was still worth a shot checking," Moose said.

"But probably just another dead end," I answered.

"Hey, we take leads where we get them," my grandfather said. "At least we got to tell your father how we felt about him."

"That's true. He doesn't resent our relationship, by the way."

"You came out and asked him?" Moose asked.

"Why not?"

"What did he say, exactly?" Moose wanted to know.

"He was happy that we'd each found someone who could stand us," I said with a grin.

"Well, he's not wrong there."

Chapter 13

After my folks and Jack left the diner, I told Martha, "You've had a long day. Why don't you and Moose take off and get some rest this evening? I'm going to need you again some tomorrow, if you're willing, and I don't want to completely wear you out today."

"You know that you can call me anytime," Martha said, though I noticed that she didn't try to talk me out of sending her home.

"And I want to be able to keep doing that, but I've got things here covered tonight."

"Thank you." She saw Moose across the room swapping lies with Lefty Hicks and called out, "Are you ready to go yet, you old fool?"

"You're going to have to be a lot more specific than that, or half the men in here are going to try to leave with you, Martha," Lefty replied.

She laughed at that. "Lefty, there's no old fool like mine. The rest of you are just pale imitations of the real thing."

"That stings, Martha. Remember once upon a time you preferred me over this fellow here. We went to the Spring Dance together in middle school."

Moose shook his head. "You may have gone there together, but she went home with me, Lefty. You always seem to forget that part of the story."

"That's because you kidnapped her," Lefty said. "Can you think of any *other* reason she'd choose you over me?"

"I can think of dozens," Moose said with a smile.

My grandfather slapped his old friend on the back, and then Moose approached Martha, extending his arm. "My lady, if you're ready, let's go home."

Martha kissed his cheek, and I could swear that she blushed a little as she did so. "You never change, do you?"

"I thought you loved me just the way I was," Moose said.

"In the beginning I might have changed a few things if I could have, but truth be told, I've gotten used to you over the years, warts and all."

"If there's a compliment in there, I'm having a hard time spotting it, but I'll just assume you meant there to be one, and I'm going to take it."

After my grandparents were gone, the diner seemed positively restrained. Greg was in the kitchen working his magic, and I was waiting on customers and ringing them up when they finished eating. We were a good team, but there wasn't time for us to chat for more than a brief word now and then.

Greg and I were closing up for the night when I saw that we were about to have one last customer. If it had been anyone else, I would have turned him away, but this happened to be someone I was pretty keen to speak with.

"Do you have a minute, Victoria? I know it's closing time, but this conversation might be beneficial to you as well as to me."

"Sure thing, Sheriff Croft. Come on in. I'm sure that Greg won't mind."

"Hi, Sheriff," Greg said as he came out front. "Don't mind me. I've got more work to do in back."

"I won't be long," the sheriff told him.

"Take your time. I'm working on a new cobbler recipe, so I don't mind the extra time in the kitchen to experiment."

"You're kidding, right? I love your cobbler just the way it is," the sheriff said.

"Thanks, but it can *always* be better. Everything can, as a matter of fact. Well, not everything. Fried eggs are as good as they are ever going to get. Bacon, too. That stuff is unbelievable."

"I thought you cut bacon out of your diet completely," I told my husband.

"Every now and then I have a nibble," he confessed. "Not more than once a week, and never an entire piece. Victoria, I have to make sure that our supplier is keeping up with the quality of the products we serve. I owe it to our customers."

"Do you taste the tomatoes every week, too?" I asked him with a grin. My husband loved ketchup, but hated tomatoes, so I knew that it really wasn't a fair question.

"I take a bite, but then I spit it out every time," he said.

"Then I'll forgive you your bacon."

Once Greg was back in the kitchen and I had the diner's front door locked, I poured two cups of coffee. Sliding one in front of the sheriff at the bar where he'd taken a seat, I grabbed another that was close by and took a sip of my own cup. "You can't pay for this, since I was getting ready to throw it out anyway. I'd better warn you, though. It's been sitting for a while, so it might be a bit strong."

"No need to apologize. That's the way I like it. Sorry I didn't get back to you earlier. I had something that I had to take care of."

"Another homicide?" I asked.

"No, nothing nearly that dramatic, but I couldn't afford to ignore it. Why did you call me, anyway?"

"Unless I'm wrong, which I don't think I am, I can eliminate at least one suspect for you, and maybe even two."

"I have to tell you, you've got my attention," he said as he pushed his cup away. "Let's hear it."

"Today I overheard Cal Davies at The Harbor Inn extorting money from Jessie Blackstone."

"And that's supposed to prove them both innocent of murder? I don't get it."

"Give me a chance to explain first," I said. "Cal extorted money from Jessie because he witnessed a fight that she had with Gordon that incriminated her. When she refused to give him any more money, he changed strategies and told her that if she didn't pay him more, he'd keep her alibi to himself, and she could rot in jail for all that he cared."

"How would Cal know what Jessie was up to at the time of the murder?" the sheriff asked me as he pulled the cup back, and then clearly had second thoughts about taking another sip. Well, I'd warned him. It was strong enough to get up and walk away.

"Evidently Cal was up to something in the corridor near her room during the entire window of time that Gordon was murdered. She was inside all afternoon, and he swears that he can testify to it. That lets her off the hook, and him too, if he's on your list."

"He's not, although Cal has certainly crossed the line enough in the past to make someone else angry enough to kill him. I know that Cal isn't squeaky clean by any means, but he's gone too far this time."

"What are you going to do to him?" I asked.

"Me personally? Nothing. I'll go out and talk to him, and Jessie as well, to confirm their stories. Once I'm satisfied that he really can provide her with an alibi for the murder, I'll casually mention to the owner what Cal has been up to."

"Will he get fired?" I asked. I hated the thought that I was going to be an instrument in getting the man dismissed from his job, but I didn't see any way that it could be helped.

"It wouldn't surprise me. At the very least, I imagine that he'll get transferred to a post far less prestigious than the one that he has now. Don't worry about Cal. I have a hunch that he'll land on his feet, no matter what happens to him. He's the kind of guy that could fall into a barrel of slop and pull out a diamond ring."

"Do you believe him when he claims to alibi Jessie?"

"This time I do, because I understand his strategy. In order to give Jessie a real alibi, he has to admit what he was up to, and I've got a hunch that it's nothing he wants known. That's why he tried to use the fight first. He could do that without any repercussions for himself."

"That's something, then," I said. "Have you been able to narrow the time of death any further?"

He nodded. "We can say with near certainty that Gordon Murphy was killed between two and three in the afternoon."

"Is the coroner that good in pinpointing times of death these days?" I asked.

"We used his preliminary estimate, and then we were able to narrow the timeline by finding witnesses who passed directly by the scene of the crime before the murder. Gordon was found a minute before three, and we have the last known empty sighting of the spot where he was killed a little after two. That should help matters, and I'm hoping that some of our suspects will be able to refine their whereabouts a little clearer now. So far, we've gotten mostly lousy alibis."

"How about your list of suspects? Would you care to compare notes with Moose and me?" I asked him with a grin.

Sheriff Croft laughed. "Tell you what I am willing to do. Why don't you tell me who made your list, and I'll add anything that's relevant whenever I can."

"I couldn't call Moose at home to invite him to join us, could I?" I asked. I hated the idea of doing too much without my grandfather, and I knew that he wouldn't appreciate me sharing the details of our investigation with the sheriff without him.

Sheriff Croft glanced at his watch, and then he frowned. "I'm sorry, I'm honestly not trying to exclude him, but I don't have that kind of time. I'm in the middle of an active murder investigation, remember?"

"I'm not about to forget it," I said. "Don't worry about it. I'll catch him up later. Where should I start?"

"A list of names might be nice," he said.

"Okay, here goes." As I started to share our list with him, I decided to add motives as well to the mix. It was time to be open and honest about the folks we were looking at as potential murderers, and why they'd made it onto our radar.

"First, there's Ellen, and her connections to Gordon. I believe in my heart that Ellen herself didn't do it, but I admit that I'm prejudiced in her favor. Still, the man came to town threatening to take her children away, so that's most likely motive enough for anyone."

"Actually, I'm kind of surprised to hear you say that, Victoria," the sheriff said.

I tried not to get upset as I explained, "Moose and I are

doing our best to look at this case rationally, so we're leaving ourselves open to every possibility. My loyalty to Ellen has nothing to do with her name being on our list. I will never believe that she killed Gordon, no matter how strong her motivation might have been, not unless she tells me herself, and even then, I'm not sure."

He laughed. "I would expect nothing less from you. I think it's a compliment to your progress as an investigator that you've got her on your list at all."

"Is she on yours too?" I asked softly.

The sheriff nodded slightly, but it was clear that it gave him no joy to do so. "Motivation can be a strong factor in murder. Who else made your list?"

"Let's see. Based on their proximity to Ellen, we've got Robert and Opal Hightower, and Wayne, her boyfriend. Their motives are all the same. They love Ellen, and every single one of them wants to protect her."

"Do you really believe that either one of her parents might have actually done it?" the sheriff asked, his coffee now completely forgotten.

"There's something funny about those two. On two separate occasions in the last few days, each one has implied that the other *might* have done it."

"You've got to love that kind of loyalty and devotion," the sheriff said. "That reminds me. One of my officers found Opal's jacket. There was no blood, just paint that matched the sample from one of the benches we took. I'm afraid that's a dead end."

"No worries. It's not the first one I've faced in this investigation," I said.

"Who else is on your list of suspects?" the sheriff asked. "Or is that it?"

"No, we have two more names: Sam Jackson and Mitchell Cobb. Evidently there was some really bad blood between Gordon and Sam Jackson. Jackson keeps claiming that everything was settled, and that all debts were repaid, but I'm not sure that I believe him."

"I've got my eye on him as well," the sheriff said. "But what's this about Mitchell Cobb? That's news to me."

"It appears that Mitchell seems to have fixated on Ellen since she threw him over in high school for Gordon."

The sheriff whistled softly. "That's a long time to keep a flame alive *and* hold a grudge."

"Hey, in matters of the heart, there's not always an expiration date."

"Isn't that the truth? I've seen some crazy things done in the past in the name of love."

"I bet you have. So, I've laid my cards all out on the table. Now, what can you tell me?"

"Do you mean that I haven't already shared enough?" he asked with a soft smile.

"That's exactly what I mean," I said. "Come on, we're on the same side here, and you know it."

"Victoria, that's the *only* reason that I put up with your meddling," he said. I might have reproached him for the dig, but I decided at the last second that might not be in my best interest. The sheriff smiled outright when he saw that I wasn't going to react. "Okay, now I'm officially impressed."

"Because I kept my temper in check?" I asked.

"You've got to admit that you've given me grief for a lot less in the past," he said.

"What can I say? It's the new me."

"I know enough not to comment on that one way or the other. Let's see. What do I know that you don't?" He tapped the table for a long fifteen seconds before he said, "Believe it or not, our lists are more similar than you might think. I can't share much, but let me say this. There's not a soul on your list that doesn't have the potential to be the killer that we're both looking for."

"Is there anyone on your list that didn't make ours?" I asked. The sheriff's praise was all well and good, but I needed more than that if Moose and I were going to have any success solving this case.

"There's one woman you missed," he said. "I can't tell

you her name, or anything else about her, but after we narrowed down the time of death, I have a hunch that she's going to be alibied nicely."

"Is she local?" I asked. "Come on. At least give me that."

"Sorry, but not even that," the sheriff said as he stood. "Tell you what. If she doesn't have an alibi from two to three, you and I will talk again."

"I can live with that," I said, though it was less than ideal. Still, if Gordon was seeing another woman on the side, she'd somehow managed to slip under *our* radar completely. I hadn't heard anything about Gordon cheating on Jessie before their nuptials, so I really didn't have any reason to be upset that the sheriff was holding out on me.

As he headed for the door, I unlocked it, and Sheriff Croft added, "You and Moose be careful out there, Victoria. I don't have to remind you that there's a killer somewhere among us that's still on the loose."

"No, I'm well aware of it, and so is my partner in crime."

"I'll be in touch," he said.

I held the door open for a second. "You know where to find me most of the time," I said.

"And when I don't, that's telling, too, isn't it? Good night."

"Good night, Sheriff."

After I locked the door back, I went into the kitchen.

"How goes the great cobbler experiment?" I asked Greg as he frowned at his mixing bowl.

"This batter is completely unacceptable," he said as he emptied the mess into the trashcan. "Don't worry, I'll get it sooner or later."

I kissed his cheek. "I know you will. What do you say we clean up, balance the register, and go home? I could use a good long soak in the tub before bed tonight."

"Tell you what. I'll make us some dinner while you do, and after we eat, you can do the dishes and I'll take a hot shower."

"A bath is better," I said, sparking an ongoing debate we'd

been having since we were first married. My husband,
reasonable in most things, hated baths, and loved showers
instead. Evidently he'd despised being forced into the tub as
a young boy, and the animosity had never ceased.

"Says you," Greg said as he kissed the tip of my nose.
"How much do you want to bet that I finish cleaning up
before you do?"

"That's not fair, and you know it," I said. "I love my
grandmother with all of my heart, but balancing a register
after she's worked a day can be a real challenge."

"Why else do you think I'd offer to bet?" Greg asked.

The joke ended being on him, though.

The register totals were so far out of balance that he ended
up cleaning the dining room after he finished the kitchen. It
was the only way he could be sure that I'd be free to go home
with him. At least he was a good sport about the whole thing.

Unfortunately, our dinner together at home was about to
be delayed by another development that we didn't know
about yet.

Chapter 14

Someone was sitting on our front porch when we arrived home, and I grabbed Greg's arm before he pulled into our driveway. "Somebody's sitting there in the dark waiting for us," I said.

"Should I call the police?" Greg asked as he reached for his cellphone.

"I'm not sure. I'd really like to see who it is first."

My husband shook his head. "Victoria, this isn't the time to be taking any chances. There's a murderer loose in town, and I don't want us to be the next victims."

"Back up first and shine your headlights onto the porch," I said. "Hang on. There's no need to do that after all. Whoever was just sitting there moved." As the motion-detecting light kicked on, I took a deep breath. "There's no need to call the police, Greg. It's just Ellen."

"What's she doing here?" my husband asked me.

"I don't know. Why don't you go ahead and pull in? Once you park the car, we can ask her ourselves."

"I can do that," Greg said.

Ellen walked toward us once we parked, and by the time I got out of the car, she was at my door. "Hey there. What brings you here?"

"Victoria, I need to talk to you," she said solemnly.

"Fine. I'm all yours. Would you like to come in?"

Ellen shook her head. "Could we just sit out on the porch?"

"Sure thing," I said.

Greg smiled at Ellen, and then he said, "If you two will excuse me, I'll get started on dinner. Ellen, you're more than welcome to stay and eat with us. I always make too much, anyway."

"Thanks, but Mom already fed me," she said.

"Then I'll leave you to it," he said as he went inside. Greg knew when I needed some privacy, and he always respected it when I was working on a murder case.

"Now, what's going on?"

"I'm worried about everyone around me," Ellen said, the words tumbling out of her in a rush.

"Is there anything in particular that's bothering you?"

"Mom and Dad are both acting so weird that it's like I don't even know them anymore. Add that to Wayne's posturing around Gordon, and I'm under more stress right now than any one woman should have to endure."

"How are the kids holding up?" I asked.

"They just lost their father, so they're both upset, but Gordon hasn't really been all that much a factor in their daily lives for years, so they're having trouble dealing with it. It's almost as though it happened to a stranger; do you know what I mean?"

"Honestly, I don't have a clue. I've never been in that kind of position before."

"And you never want to be, either. They're both strong. They'll bounce back, once a little time has passed. I just wish that I could say the same thing about myself."

"You're tough, too. Never forget that. It hasn't been easy what you've been doing over the past several years. You've held it together better than *I* ever would have managed."

"Victoria, you're the strongest woman I know. You would have handled things just fine on your own."

"I'm not at all sure that's true, but I appreciate hearing that you believe it. So, tell me a little more about your folks, and Wayne, too. What exactly is going on with them?"

"Mom and Dad are both tiptoeing around each other, and it's taken me a while to figure it out, but I think I know why."

I had my own suspicions about their behavior, but I decided not to share them and find out what conclusion Ellen had reached on her own.

"Tell me," I said.

"I believe that they each think the other one might have done it," she said.

"That's what I think, too," I said.

Ellen looked at me sharply. "You've seen it, too?"

"You know that your mother confessed to killing Gordon already, don't you?"

She was shocked by the mere suggestion. "Please tell me that you're kidding."

"I wish I could," I said as I relayed the details of what had happened to her. "She couldn't remember how she killed him, though."

"He was struck from behind with a pipe," Ellen said. "You'd think that would be kind of hard to forget, especially if you're the one who did it."

"I'm sure that her confession was motivated by love," I said. "She was just trying to protect you."

"How, by making me look guilty?" Ellen asked. "That's just like Mom, trying to take every bullet that's meant for me."

"Both of your parents love you," I said.

"I know they do. As a matter of fact, I'm surprised that Dad hasn't confessed, too."

"Maybe he was waiting until he found out what really happened to Gordon so he could get his facts straight," I said with a grin.

"You could be right," Ellen said. "Save us from our parents, right?"

"I don't know. I think we both got pretty lucky in that respect."

"So do I," Ellen said.

"Tell me about Wayne," I suggested.

She let out a grunt of frustration. "He's been trying to be macho ever since Gordon first hit him. I think the blow to his pride stung a lot more than the punch. I'm concerned that he might have done something drastic to regain his self-respect. The day Gordon was murdered, I tried to tell Wayne that I didn't care if he could win a fistfight or not, but I don't think that he believed me."

"You told me earlier that you were with him the afternoon of the murder. Do you remember what time it might have been?" Ellen had some rather large holes in her alibi, significant time that she'd spent alone on the day of the murder.

"Like I said before, I had Dad pick the kids up," she admitted. "I've been doing that every so often so that Wayne and I could have some time together. I've been putting together some nice picnic baskets, and we've been stealing a little time together every day."

"Ellen, this is very important. When *exactly* did you see him the day Gordon was murdered?"

She thought about it for nearly thirty seconds before she answered, and then she said, "We got together about one forty five, and Wayne had to get back to the shop by three fifteen. Normally he's never gone that long, but I needed him that day, and he was willing to take some extra time off so I could talk things out."

"That's wonderful news," I said as I reached for my cellphone.

"Yes, he's an excellent shoulder to cry on." She looked at me oddly as I started to dial. "What's going on? Who are you going to call and tell *that* to?"

"I'm phoning the sheriff. This is perfect. It's going to take you two off his list."

"I don't understand," Ellen said.

"They've been able to narrow the window for Gordon's murder since the last time we spoke. He was killed between two and three in the afternoon, and from what you said, you two were together the entire time. There's just one thing before I call the sheriff and tell him, though. Is there anyone else who can substantiate the fact that you two were together the entire time?"

Ellen frowned as she thought about it. "We were at the park, so I doubt that anyone could verify it one way or the other. Sorry. I'm not going to be able to do you much good."

That was disappointing, but I wasn't ready to give up yet. "Think hard, Ellen. That park is never empty, especially on a beautiful afternoon like the day of the murder was. Are you telling me that no one can confirm that you were there together?"

"No one," she said, and then Ellen frowned. "Hang on a second. That's not entirely true. There's one witness who was near us the entire time. Whether she noticed us at all is up for debate, though."

"What's her name?" I asked. This could be the one crucial piece of evidence that would get her off the hook.

"It was Crazy Betty," she said. "She was doing crossword puzzles on the bench closest to our picnic blanket the entire time. You know how obsessed she gets over things."

I did, indeed. Betty Cliburn, affectionately known as Crazy Betty around town, had a streak of obsessive/compulsive disorder that was just below the level requiring medication. When she narrowed her laser focus to a new hobby or interest, she lived and breathed it with everything that she had. Then one day, without rhyme or reason, she'd drop it cold and never revisit it again. So far, she'd knitted until her fingers bled, read everything written by a dozen different cozy mystery authors, and she was now going through crossword puzzles in a blaze of speed. "It's how she copes with Cliff's death," I said. "Betty has never really learned how to get along without him."

"I don't know if she saw us or not, but we were there, Victoria."

"I'm sure the sheriff can track her down and ask her," I said. "You don't have any objections about me calling him, do you?"

"Are you kidding? If you can get me off his list of murder suspects, I'll sing your praises to the world, and I'd be forever grateful."

"Well, save your singing voice, because I haven't done *anything* yet," I said. "Give me one second."

I finished dialing the sheriff's number, and he finally

picked up after six rings.

"Is this a bad time?" I asked him.

"No, it's fine. What's new since the last time we spoke, though? Surely nothing substantial has changed in the past half hour."

"You'd be surprised. I now have an alibi for Ellen and Wayne, but it's going to take a little legwork on your part to confirm."

"That's what we're good at," the sheriff said. "You know me. I'm not afraid of a little hard work."

"Okay, here goes. Ellen and Wayne snuck away to the park from one forty-five to three fifteen on the afternoon of the murder to have some time together. Ellen needed a shoulder to cry on, and Wayne was more than happy to supply it."

"That's all well and good, but unless someone else saw them there together, it's not going to do any of us much good."

"That's the thing. Betty Cliburn was on a park bench nearby doing her crossword puzzles. Ellen swears that the woman was there the entire time," I explained.

"She might have been sharing their blanket, but that doesn't mean that Betty saw them. You know how she gets when she's working on something."

"You're still going to ask her, though, aren't you?" I asked.

"Of course I will. I'm just saying that you shouldn't get your hopes up."

"Sorry, but it's a bit too late for that."

"I'll talk to her right now. Do you have anything else for me?"

I thought about conveying what Ellen had told me about her parents, but I really didn't have anything to share on that front yet. "Hey, you said it yourself. We haven't been apart all that long."

"You can't blame me for asking," he replied.

"Would you do me a favor?" I asked him while I still had

him on the line.

"Maybe," he answered cagily. I knew the sheriff was too savvy to make a blanket promise without hearing what it was first.

"Don't worry. This is an easy one. I'd just appreciate a telephone call after you talk to Betty, one way or the other. It would be nice to know if Ellen and Wayne are off your list."

"I can do that," the sheriff said. "It might be late, though. If I can't find her tonight, I might have to ask her in the morning."

"Just as long as you let me know what's going on, we're good."

"Okay, I'll see what I can do. And Victoria?"

"Yes?"

"Thanks for the tip."

"You're welcome," I said, but it was to a dead phone. The sheriff had already hung up.

"What did he say?" Ellen asked me.

"He's going to talk to Betty, and then he'll touch base with me. It might be tomorrow, though, so we need to be patient."

"I can wait as long as I need to," she said. "I just hope that she saw us there. It would simplify so many things if she did."

"I hope so, too. Ellen, are you sure that you don't want to come in for a bite, and some company? You know that Greg wouldn't mind."

"No, I'd better be going," she said as she stood. "I've stayed away from my family as long as I dare. They need me right now."

"Give them my love, would you?"

"I will, and thanks for that from me," she said.

"You're very welcome," I answered sincerely.

After Ellen was gone, I thought about the most recent developments with the case. Ellen and Wayne might be off the hook if Betty confirmed their alibi, but her parents were still active members of my suspect list, and what she'd told me hadn't eased my mind, either.

Chapter 15

"You're not going in there," I heard a voice say threateningly as Sam Jackson stepped out of the shadows and tried to keep me from going into The Charming Moose the next morning.

"It's going to take more than you to stop me," I said as I started to push past him. It was just before six a.m., and there wasn't much traffic out. To most folks driving past the diner, it probably looked as though Sam and I were just having ourselves a nice little chat.

They would have been mistaken.

"That's where you're wrong," Sam said. "Listen, we can do this the hard way, or we can do it easy. In the end, it makes no difference to me."

"I'm not going to make killing me easy for you," I said harshly. "If you want my life, you're going to have to fight for it."

"*Kill* you? Where did you get that idea?" Jackson asked me, clearly surprised by my reaction.

"You ambush me at my diner in the early hours when no one else is around and you threaten me," I said. "Why wouldn't I think that you meant me harm? I'm just telling you that if that's your goal, I'm not about to make it easy for you."

"I want to talk. That's it, Victoria. Just talk."

"Then wait one minute for me to get set up inside and then come on in," I said as I pushed past him. I had my keys out and the door unlocked before he could process the new information. I thought about slamming it shut behind me and locking him on the outside, but what if he was telling the truth? I had a suspect who was willing to discuss Gordon Murphy's murder with me. Talking was what I did best. After I overcame my impulse to protect my mother and myself, I walked in back and smiled at Mom.

"You got here early," I said as I hung my jacket up.

"Your husband isn't the only one in the family who likes to play with recipes," she said. "I thought that I'd have a little fun."

I took a deep breath, and as I did, I smelled something divine baking. "Is that cornbread?"

"Jalapeno cheddar cornbread, to be exact," she said. "I'm not sure how it's going to taste, but it smells magnificent, doesn't it?"

"I'd *love* to try some," I said.

Mom looked at the timer. "Four more minutes, and then I'll join you. It's not too early in the day for spicy cornbread, is it?"

"Is it ever too early for something delicious?" I asked.

"You've got a point there."

I heard the front door open, so I told Mom, "I need to go back out front."

"Go, take care of them. Don't worry; I'll save you a piece."

"At least one," I said with a smile.

I walked back out front, and I found that Sam Jackson had already taken a seat at the bar. "Listen, I'm sorry about that," he said, sounding a little embarrassed as he spoke. "I get used to dealing with a certain type, and sometimes I forget how to treat civilians."

"Are you at war?" I asked him.

"Sometimes it feels that way. Victoria, I'm not going to pretend that I'll miss Gordon Murphy, but that doesn't mean that I killed him."

"It doesn't mean that you didn't, either," I said.

Jackson just shook his head. "When did you get to be such a hard-nose?" he asked. "You're not at all what I expected."

"I've investigated murder before," I said. "It takes something out of you, and it leaves something else behind."

"I can see that," he said. "Listen. I need you to stop sniffing around my life. It's not good for business."

"I'm sorry, but I'm afraid that can't be helped," I said.

"Until and unless I get a usable alibi from you, you have to stay on my list of suspects. You and the victim had a history of bad blood between you, and what's more, you've never tried to deny it. The only way you're going to convince me that you had nothing to do with Gordon's murder is to provide me and the police with a solid alibi."

"What if I told you I was doing something somewhere else at the time of the murder?" he asked me pointedly. "Would that get you off my back?"

"It would be a start. Where were you?"

"That's where it gets a little sticky," Jackson said with a sigh. "I was doing something I'd just as soon the police not know I was involved in. If I tell you, you're going to go to them with it, aren't you?"

"I *might* be able to make an exception," I said. "But I would have to have solid proof."

"I understand that. But listen, I need your word that you're not going to go to Sheriff Croft with this. It could be bad for me if you did, and I wouldn't like that." The threat in his voice was again very real, and I felt myself shiver a little at the thought of Sam Jackson's possible retribution.

"There's no need for you to say anything else," I said.

"Because you don't believe me?" he asked.

"As a matter of fact, I do. Your willingness to incriminate yourself even to me is enough to convince me that you're most likely telling the truth."

"But you aren't persuaded, are you?"

"Think about it. Let's say that an associate of yours calls me and tells me that you were in Hickory robbing a bank when Gordon was being murdered. How can I believe that he's telling me the truth, and not just following your orders?"

"Well, in the first place, I don't rob banks," Jackson said. "It's too dangerous, and there are better ways to get a payday than sticking a gun under somebody's nose."

That was good to know, but my point was still valid. "It was just an example. What I'm saying is that anyone who vouches for you is by definition suspicious in my mind. I'll tell you what I'm willing to do. I won't actively pursue any lead regarding you unless I have more reason than I do right now to believe that you might have had something to do with Gordon Murphy's murder."

"That's the best that I'm going to get out of you, isn't it?" he asked after showing me a brief frown.

"Sorry, but it is."

"Then I can live with it, for now," he said. "If you want my opinion, I know a guy you should be looking at for this murder."

I expected him to say Wayne's name, so I was quite surprised when he mentioned Mitchell Cobb. "The man's obsessed with your waitress. That's all he can talk about every single time I see him. I'll tell you something. We've been friends for a *long* time, and Ellen's the *only* woman that he's ever talked about. If you ask me, he's the one who needs the attention of the police, not me." Was Jackson giving me a real clue that Mitchell might be involved, or was he simply feeding me his friend's name to divert suspicion away from himself? I wasn't sure, but it was something that I was determined to find out.

As Sam Jackson stood in order to leave the diner, I asked, "Would you like some breakfast while you're here?"

I never expected him to agree, but after a moment's thought, he shrugged and said, "Sure, why not? How about a stack of hotcakes? I haven't had good ones in a while."

"Then you're in for a real treat. My mother makes the best flapjacks around."

"We'll just see about that," he said.

Four minutes after placing Jackson's order, I picked up his pancakes, grabbed a container of syrup and a pat of butter, and delivered the feast to him. After he added the butter and syrup, he cut off a single bite and savored it as though it was an expensive steak and not a bargain stack of pancakes.

"Your mother is an artist," he said with a grin.

"We like to think so."

After he was finished, he tipped as much as the check was

for.

I clucked at him, and then I said, "That's entirely too much."

"It's not for you," he said with the hint of a smile. "It's for your mother."

"Cooks don't usually get tips," I said.

"Well, this one deserves it."

Jackson left the restaurant, and after I gave my mother his tip, she smiled and tucked it into her apron. "What a nice young man he must have been."

I thought about telling her the handful of rumors I'd heard about Sam Jackson, but I decided there was no reason to ruin the happy mood she was in. "He surely liked your pancakes."

"Then he's got good taste, if nothing else," she said with a smile.

"I'd have to agree with that," I said.

After I walked back up front and put his cup and plate in the bin for dirty dishes, I wiped the counter down and waited for our next visitor of the day.

Hopefully he wouldn't be as combative as Jackson had been.

I thought about what he'd told me, and I realized that I'd told him the truth.

For now, I'd cross his name off our list.

But I was going to use a pencil instead of a pen, just in case he'd been lying to me.

Who knew for sure, anyway? Suspects had lied to me before, and I knew that it would happen again, as long as Moose and I continued to investigate murder.

"Wow, this place is right out of the fifties, isn't it?" a thin older man with a ready smile asked me as he walked into the diner an hour later.

"We like it," I said.

"Oh, I do, too." He stuck out his hand. "My name is Curtis Trane."

"Hello, Curtis. I'm Victoria Nelson."

"Victoria, tell your owner that I love this place."

"You just did," I replied. The man's bright attitude was infectious, and I found myself smiling right back at him. "Sit anywhere you'd like. We don't take reservations."

He winked broadly at me. "In that case, I'll take a seat at the bar. That's where all the action is in this kind of place, isn't it?"

"I'm afraid that if you've come here for excitement, you're going to be disappointed."

"I can't imagine that's true at all. If you have time to join me, I'd love the company."

We were in a lull at the moment, with just a few diners lingering over their coffee and swapping stories. "I can't promise you *all* of my attention, but I'll do what I can." Just to make sure he wasn't getting the wrong idea, I added, "My husband works the grill later, but my mom is in charge of the kitchen now, so everything on the menu is good."

"Then, what's spectacular?" he asked. "I'm in the mood to be wowed."

"Order the pancakes, then," I said. "I know, it might seem like a rather ordinary thing to have in a diner, but folks come from miles around to have my mother's hotcakes."

"Which is it?"

"What do you mean?"

"You just called them pancakes and hotcakes in nearly the same breath."

"The terms are interchangeable, at least here. We also call them flapjacks on occasion, but no matter the name, they are guaranteed to be delicious."

"Then I'll take a stack, and a glass of orange juice," he said without even looking at his menu. "Feel free to place an order for yourself, on my tab."

"Thanks, but I'll just have juice. If I ate my mother's pancakes every day, I wouldn't be able to fit through the front door before too long."

He patted his lean stomach. "I believe I can handle them."

"Coming right up," I said.

I gave the order to Mom as I said, "Make them good. I've been bragging about you."

"No pressure there, then," she said with a smile.

"You have nothing to worry about. No one can touch your pancakes; not even Greg."

"Don't let him hear you say that. As a matter of fact, I like his more, myself."

"That's because you're both your own worst critics."

"Maybe so," Mom said as she finished the order and plated them. "There you go, Moose's Best."

"Mom's Best, you mean," I said with a wink.

"No matter who's working the grill, everything we serve represents the diner."

"I'll be sure to let him know that," I said with a laugh.

"There you go," I said as I slid the plate in front of him. After getting him the fixings, and a juice for each of us, I took a seat beside him and watched him eat. If he was anything like Sam Jackson had been, he was about to smile, and I wanted to see it.

There was no grin, or much of any reaction, though.

"You don't like them?" I asked.

"No, they're quite good," he said.

"But you've had better," I added.

"No, I can say without a doubt that they are the very best I've ever tasted."

"Then why the long face?" I was honestly curious why this happy man had just gone quiet.

"I'm sorry," he said as he stood abruptly. "I'm not feeling well."

He hadn't paid for his meal, but that honestly wasn't my concern at all. "Curtis, can I call someone for you?"

"I'm afraid at this stage, there's nothing anyone can do for me." He stumbled out of the restaurant, and I was so worried about him that I followed him out into the parking lot. Curtis shouldn't be driving himself anywhere if he was feeling that bad.

I needn't have worried about that, though. There was a

long black limousine waiting, and a sturdy young man ready at the door. Curtis got in, and before I could reach them, he drove off.

"What was that all about?" I asked myself, but since I didn't have an answer, I went back inside and quickly forgot all about him. As I cleared his place setting, I found a small plastic pickle beside his plate that I was certain hadn't been there before.

An hour later, the driver came into the diner, alone.

"Are you Victoria?" he asked.

"I am. How's Curtis doing? I was really worried about him."

"He's as good as he can be, considering that the doctors told him he should have been dead nine months ago."

I felt myself deflate, and I slumped down to a chair. "I don't know why I'm reacting this way. Honestly, I just met the man."

The driver smiled. "Curtis has that impact on everyone he meets. He's the finest man I've ever known, and I'm proud to call him my friend as well as my employer." The man then reached into his jacket pocket and pulled out a bill. "He felt bad about skipping out without paying, and he asked me to give you this as his way of apologizing."

I took the bill almost automatically, and it took me a second to realize that it was a hundred dollar bill. "Let me get you the change."

The man held both hands up. "Sorry. I was instructed not to take any change for the transaction."

"But this is way too much," I protested. He could have bought the next fifteen pancake breakfasts with the money.

"It's the least he can do. Ma'am, Curtis is worth millions of dollars, for all the good it's doing now when he's dying. This gives him enjoyment. You aren't going to rob him of that, are you?"

"You're good," I said. "You know my name, but I don't know yours."

"I'm Jeffrey," he said.

I stuck out my hand, and he took it in his. Jeffrey's grip was surprisingly gentle, given the size of the man. "It's good to meet you," he said.

"And you. I don't know what to do about this, Jeffrey."

"Give it away, if you'd like. Just don't make me disappoint him. I couldn't bear that, Victoria."

"Then I won't do it," I said. I had a sudden inspiration, and asked, "Would you think he'd mind if I use it to buy breakfast for the next dozen folks who come in here?"

Jeffrey smiled. "I think he'd very much enjoy it."

"Then that's what I'm going to do."

As the driver started to leave, I said, "Jeffrey, tell Curtis that it was an honor and a pleasure to meet him, and that he's welcome back at The Charming Moose anytime."

"I'll do that," Jeffrey said. "But don't get your hopes up. I don't think he's got that much time left."

I nodded sadly, and the driver added, "Don't mourn him, Victoria. If ever there was a life worth celebrating, it's his."

"Thank you. Jeffrey, can I get you anything?"

"Thanks, but I'm needed elsewhere."

He was at the door when he hesitated. "Did you find the pickle?"

"I did," I said. "Does he want it back?"

Jeffrey just smiled. "No, it's kind of his calling card. That's how his family made their money, and he gets a kick out of giving pickles away."

I laughed at the notion. "I'll keep it someplace safe, then."

After he was gone, I thought yet again about how fleeting life could be. Money was no guarantee of anything that really mattered, but I hoped that in the end, there was someone there to comfort Curtis Trane.

I felt quite a bit like Santa for the next little while, paying off the next dozen diners' tabs that came my way. I didn't tell a soul what was happening until it was time to pay, and I got to share Curtis's story again and again. Somehow, I think that he would have approved of all of the delighted smiles and laughter his kind gesture had generated. Using his money, I'd been able to spread more sunshine than shadow, and at the end of the day, what better measuring stick was there?

Chapter 16

"How's your morning been so far?" Moose asked me as he and Martha walked into the diner a little after I'd paid off the last bill.

"It's been fine," I said.

"I'm guessing that there's more to say than that. What's this I hear about you giving away free breakfasts? I know the place is yours to run as you please, Victoria, but do you honestly believe that it's a good precedent to set? Folks are going to expect free food whenever we're open."

I didn't know why it surprised me that Moose had already heard about what had happened, though he hadn't gotten the complete story. Jasper Fork was like that. Folks might not get all of the details right through the grapevine, but they got the overall picture just fine, and usually in record time, as well.

"I didn't give any food away at all," I said.

Moose's right eyebrow shot up. "Are you saying that I heard it wrong, then?"

"No, but there's a great deal more to it than that." I explained to him what had happened, and my decision about how to deal with Curtis's windfall.

I half expected my grandfather to scold me for my behavior, but when I was finished with my explanation, he nodded his agreement. "Victoria, that was precisely the right thing to do."

"I'm glad you approve," I said. "Jenny came in a few minutes ago. Are you ready to start sleuthing this morning, or is it too early to go knocking on doors?"

"I don't know that we have a lot of choice in the matter, do you? I heard that Jessie has already left town, with the sheriff's blessing. Who knows how long our other suspects are going to hang around?"

"I hadn't heard anything about that," I said. "I wonder how much she ultimately gave to Cal?"

"In the end, he got twelve thousand dollars," Moose said.

"How could you possibly know that?" I asked. My grandfather had a great many connections around Jasper Fork, but this seemed even beyond *his* scope of reach.

"Let's just say that I had a hand in getting him to return it all to her and leave it at that," Moose said with a big grin.

"Why on earth would he give any of it back?"

"Well, it was either repay the money, or face a jail sentence. It turns out that Cal was doing a great deal more than using extortion and blackmail to accumulate funds. We'll probably never know how much he made on the side in his position, but one thing's certain: he won't be making anything more there."

"Did you get him fired, Moose?"

"Let's just say that I played a small role in relocating him," Moose said. "When will people around here learn that they lie to me at their own peril?" While I knew my grandfather as a sweet man at heart, I also understood that he had an edge of steel in his heart.

"Is he staying in town?"

Moose checked his watch. "Hardly. He has another ninety-seven minutes, but he'll be long gone by then if he has any sense at all."

"I'm glad that you helped Jessie," I said.

Moose just shrugged. "She's not a bad person at heart, Victoria. She just happened to fall for the wrong man. It's hard to hold that against her, don't you think?"

I thought about how Ellen had fallen for the same man several years before. "Yes, love can be a dangerous thing, can't it?"

"Not for us, though," Moose said with a smile.

"We both got lucky, and you know it," I said, matching his grin with one of my own.

"I never denied it. So, who should we tackle first today?"

I conveyed the conversation I'd had with Sam Jackson earlier, and in particular, I stressed his concerns about Mitchell Cobb.

"I don't know why, but I still have a hard time seeing that man killing anyone," Moose said.

"I know what you mean, but Jackson was pretty adamant."

"And you believed him?" Moose asked. "Is he really off the hook in our books?"

I nodded. "I think so. Why would he take the risk of incriminating himself for another crime if he weren't telling me the truth?"

"You spoke with him; I didn't. What does your gut tell you?"

"That he didn't do it. He's not innocent, not by anyone's definition, but I'm fairly certain that he didn't kill Gordon Murphy."

"That's good enough for me, then. Who does that leave us?"

"We're still waiting to hear from the sheriff about Ellen and Wayne." I'd looked around to be sure that Ellen was in the kitchen when I'd said it. "If Crazy Betty can confirm their alibis, then they're both in the clear."

"Then we can add their names to Jessie and Cal, who are both off the hook, and according to you, we can strike Sam Jackson's name off as well."

"In pencil, though," I told Moose. "I'm willing to admit that I could be wrong about him."

"If I'm placing a bet, it's always going to be on you," my grandfather said.

"Thanks," I said. "That just leaves us with Opal, Robert, and Mitchell. I'm not afraid to admit it, Moose. I hope that Mitchell did it."

"I know. It's going to be hard to accuse either one of Ellen's parents of murder when they were just trying to protect her."

"If it is one of them, I'll get no joy from finding a killer."

"Then let's go see what Mitchell has to say for himself," Moose said.

The house was clearly rented, and the state of the yard

shouted that no homeowner lived at Mitchell Cobb's address. The grass was a good week past when it needed to be mowed, and the landscape itself was devoid of flowers or shrubs or anything ornamental that might make the place feel the least bit cozy.

I tapped on the door, and to my surprise, it opened at my touch. Who doesn't lock their door anymore in this day and age? "Hello?" I called out. "Mitchell, are you there?"

"I don't think he's home," Moose said after a few moments of waiting.

"What do you think we should do?"

"Let's go in and look around," my grandfather said.

I wasn't the least bit surprised by his suggestion. Moose liked to take chances, and a lot of the time I agreed with him. It was better to be bold and search than to wait for clues to come to us, but we were dealing with a potential killer here. Still, how many opportunities like this did we get? "Let's do it, but we have to be careful."

"Always," Moose said as he walked into the house.

Once we were inside the house, my grandfather pulled the door closed behind us. It made me feel trapped for some reason, as though he'd just shut off our only means of escape.

"Victoria, are you okay?" Moose asked me.

"I'm fine. How should we handle our search?"

"I don't know," he said. "I've got a hunch that we don't have a lot of time. I hate the idea of us splitting up, but we can cover a lot more ground if you start at the bottom and I take the top. We can work towards the center and meet back here."

"Sure, that's fine with me, as long as we reverse things. How about if I take the upstairs and you go to the basement? I've never been all that fond of the creepy things that live belowground, and you know it."

"It's a deal," he said. "Call me on your cellphone if you find anything."

"We're not going to just shout out loud for one another?" I asked with the hint of a nervous smile. That was our normal way to communicate, after all.

"No, I think the less noise we make here, the better."

"It's a deal," I said.

As I headed upstairs, I began to regret our decision to split up almost immediately. I constantly yelled at the television when Greg and I watched those Women in Peril movies they showed late at night. Sometimes the lead characters did the dumbest things, and I could never understand their motivation for putting their lives at risk, and yet here I was, doing basically the same thing that I blamed them for doing. Well, not entirely. I wasn't alone in the house, at least. My grandfather was just a phone call away, and no matter how old Moose might be, I knew that he'd have my back.

The second stair from the top creaked so loudly that I almost screamed as my foot hit the tread. If Mitchell was upstairs, I'd just announced my presence, loud and clear. I decided to play it safe, just in case he really was up there somewhere.

"Mitchell? Are you there? We heard a noise outside, so we thought we'd come check on you."

We hadn't heard anything, as a matter of fact, but I wanted some plausible deniability to the fact that my grandfather and I were actually trespassing on his property.

There was no answer, and I finally started to breathe again.

The bedrooms were rather austere, with no extraneous photographs, or anything that made it appear that someone was actually living there. I wondered how the closets would look, and the first one was normal enough, filled with men's shoes, hanging shirts and pants, and a few decent suits.

The second closet was *nothing* like that, though.

As I opened the door, a light switched on automatically, and I saw that instead of paint, the walls were papered with photographs of Ellen. There were hundreds of candid shots, dating back to when she must have been in high school, and in nearly every instance, it appeared that she wasn't even aware that she was being photographed.

I felt my breath choke in my throat. I could easily see this man as Ellen's stalker. Taking out my camera phone, I snapped a few shots, but as I looked at them, I realized that they couldn't begin to convey the overall creepiness of the space. After I had a few photos as a record, I called Moose.

"Come upstairs right now," I said in a whisper. I wanted someone else to see what I was looking at.

"I'll be right there," he said.

As I hung up the phone, I heard that top step squeak, and I knew that there was no way that Moose had made it up the stairs that quickly.

Pulling the door closed until just a crack of light peeked through, I looked out to see if Mitchell was coming into the bedroom, and when I saw him darken the doorway, I nearly cried out, solely as a reflex of panic. I managed to stifle it, though. I had to. I didn't want Mitchell catching me in that closet, but then again, I couldn't have him ambushing my grandfather, either.

I had to do something, and I had to do it fast.

Chapter 17

I looked around the closet for something that I could use as a weapon, but unfortunately, there was nothing really there. No clothes hung on the wooden rod, and no empty hangers, either.

They would have interfered with Mitchell's photo gallery, most likely.

The only thing that *was* there was the closet rod, a thick round piece of wood that looked stout enough to take a man down. I tried to pull the rod from its holders, but someone had screwed the thing in place on each end. The only way I was going to free it was with a screwdriver, something I most definitely was not carrying on me at the moment.

But I did have some change in my pocket.

Working as fast as I could, I used a dime to try to unscrew the rod from its moorings.

It was a complete and total failure.

I kept trying to free it, though, and as I did, I heard the footsteps coming closer, faster and faster.

There was nothing that I could use to fight back.

Facing the door, I decided to use the last option in my arsenal as I waited for Mitchell to open it and discover me. I might not have any weapons that I could use in my own defense, but I could still fight back. After all, I had two strong arms and legs, and I'd use them as weapons to defend myself if that was my only chance of getting out of there alive.

I knew that if Moose heard the fight, he'd race to join in, no matter how bad the odds might seem. It was entirely likely that we both would go down to a killer, but at least we wouldn't go down without fighting back.

Mitchell was nearly to the closet door now, and I could hear my heart trying to beat right out of my chest, when I heard the doorbell downstairs.

He hesitated, and then it rang again.

Who could it be?

I waited until I heard Mitchell walk down the stairs, and once I was certain that he was at the bottom, I raced out of the closet and through the spare bedroom.

Being careful to skip the squeaking stair, I made my way down, only to find Moose standing outside repeatedly ringing the bell.

Mitchell was still inside, though, and it didn't appear that he was in any mood to come out. I could stand there and listen to their conversation, but I couldn't get past Mitchell and make my way outside. I might be able to go out the back way with a little luck, but I needed a distraction in order to do it.

As I was trying to figure out the best way to slip past Mitchell, Moose did it for me.

At least I hoped that he was just acting, and that he wasn't *really* having a heart attack on Mitchell Cobb's front porch.

Chapter 18

"Moose, are you okay?" Mitchell Cobb asked as he shot out the door and knelt down beside my grandfather. It was eerie seeing Moose lying so silently on the porch, but I couldn't stop to worry about him yet. Tearing around the corner, I found the back door in the kitchen, and unlocking it as silently as I could, I slipped out and hurriedly closed it behind me.

Now it was my turn to act.

I tried to slow my breathing and my heartbeat as I rounded the corner, and keeping my voice as nonchalant as I could manage, I said, "Moose, I don't think he's here."

"Victoria, something's wrong with your grandfather," Mitchell said. "I already called 911, and they are on the way. What should I do in the meantime? I took a CPR class a few years ago, but they said that I was too rough. I don't want to break his ribs."

"I don't want that, either," I said. I brushed him aside, and got down close to Moose's mouth. "Are you okay?"

"My heart," he croaked out as he clutched his chest.

This didn't feel like acting to me. "Hang in there, Moose. The ambulance is on its way."

I was about to call my grandmother when the ambulance zoomed up the street toward us. Two husky paramedics got out, assessed Moose quickly, and I saw my grandfather whisper to one of them.

The man nodded, and as they loaded him onto the stretcher, the paramedic said, "You need to come with us."

I nodded, too, and then I told Mitchell, "I'll come back later to talk to you."

"Stay with him," Mitchell said. "That's where *you* need to be."

I got into the ambulance following Moose; before I could get settled, the driver took off down the road like a maniac.

We'd pick up my grandfather's truck later once the emergency was over.

Moose had an oxygen tube in his nose, and he looked a little pale to me as he lay there strapped to the gurney.

I nearly lost it when he sat up.

"That was close," my grandfather said as he removed the tube from his nose. He patted the EMS attendant on the shoulder. "Good job, Charlie. I almost thought for a second there that I really was having a heart attack."

"Overall, you seem healthy enough to me, but your blood pressure is a little bit high. You might want to get that checked out." He tapped on the driver's seat. "You can slow down now, Ben. Moose is going to be okay."

"Are you sure?" the younger tech asked. "He still looks a little ashen to me."

"That's more from your driving than because of his physical condition," Charlie said with a laugh.

Ben slowed down, and as the ambulance neared the diner, he pulled over to the side of the road.

"I owe you both a meal on the house," Moose said. "Do you have time to collect it now?"

"As a matter of fact, we were just getting ready to go on our lunch break," Charlie said. "I assume you had your own reasons for the impromptu chauffeur service."

"It's nothing that I can really talk about, but trust me when I tell you that it *was* important. Now, come on in and let's get you two fed."

"Ben, you wouldn't mind parking your rig down the street a little, would you?" I asked.

He smiled at me. "I get it. You don't want an ambulance parked in front of your diner, do you?"

"Do you mind?" I asked him.

"No, I completely understand. Why don't you and your grandfather go on and get out, and we'll park somewhere else. See you in a few."

"Thanks again," Moose said.

After we got out of the ambulance, they drove up the

street, and I turned to my grandfather before we went inside. "I've got to admit that was fast thinking on your part. You really saved my bacon in there. What were you going to do if you didn't know the EMTs?"

"Why, then, I would have had a false alarm by the time we got to the hospital. Victoria, I had to get you out of there, and I didn't know what else I could do."

"Hey, don't get me wrong; I'm not scolding you. I think it was brilliant, and I'll praise you more once I get over the little heart attack of my own that you just gave me. Seeing you sprawled out on that porch is something that's going to haunt me for years."

"Don't worry. I'm in no rush to leave you, or Martha," he said with a grin. "I'm sorry that I scared you, and especially since it was all in vain."

"But it wasn't," I told him. "You'll never believe what I found upstairs."

"Tell me," he said.

"He's got a photo collage of Ellen's life in there," I said.

"How many pictures are we talking about?" Moose asked.

"Hundreds," I said.

"Then I'm going to call the sheriff."

"Moose, he can't just barge in there like we did. He needs a warrant."

"Then he'll get one," Moose said. "Victoria, that was too close a call. If Mitchell had caught you up there snooping around in his closet, I don't want to even think about what might have happened."

"We don't have to," I said as I patted his hand. "Let *me* call the sheriff." As the EMTs approached on foot, I added, "Set them up inside while I take care of this."

He nodded, and the three of them went into The Charming Moose, all of them as thick as thieves. It appeared that Moose had made a new friend in Ben. How did the man do it? He could go to a house fire and come back with a firefighter as his new buddy.

I got the sheriff on the line, and I was happy when he

picked up on the second ring.

"How's Moose doing?" was the first thing he asked me, before I could get a single word out.

"He's fine. Why do you ask?"

"I heard about his heart attack over the radio," the sheriff said. "I'm on my way to the hospital right now, so just hold tight."

I was touched by the sheriff's reaction, but I had to stop him before he compounded the misconception that Moose was in trouble. "He's okay. It was all just a ploy."

Sheriff Croft clearly didn't like my explanation. "Explain yourself."

"We were at Mitchell Cobb's place. Before you yell at me, it's important to know that the door was unlocked when we got there."

"That doesn't excuse you both trespassing," the sheriff said.

"Slap my wrist later, okay? The man's got an upstairs closet with more pictures of Ellen than *anybody* should rightfully have. He's obsessed with her."

"What do you propose I do about it?" the sheriff asked. "I can't break in without losing my job and going to jail. You aren't immune from arrest, too; you know that, don't you?"

"Go to his house, and ask him if you can look around. You're a persuasive guy. You can do it."

"Why should I?" he asked.

"Listen, I understand that you're upset with Moose and me, but you can't let that get in the way of catching a killer."

"He doesn't have to let me in. You know that, don't you?"

"Can it hurt to ask?" I questioned him.

"I suppose not. I'm nearly there anyway. Sit tight. I'll get back to you."

After we hung up, I went inside and waited for his call. Moose was regaling the entire diner with his close brush with death, clearly enjoying every moment of it. Only Martha was frowning in his direction. I joined her at the register.

"He'll turn anything into a story, won't he?" I asked.

"I had hoped that he'd outgrow it someday, but it appears that those wishes were all in vain."

"You've got to love him," I said. "He drives me crazy sometimes. I can't imagine how you've managed it all of these years."

"Patience, prayer, and perseverance," she said. Martha patted my hand as she looked into my eyes. "Did he give you an awful fright?"

"There's no denying it, but he also might have saved my life. Take it easy on him, okay?"

"I'm not making any promises," she said with a grin, and I knew that they were going to be all right.

My phone rang, and I stepped back outside to take the call. It had been fifteen minutes, barely enough time for the sheriff to search Mitchell's house, and I felt my spirits sag. "Hello?"

"It's Croft. Nothing."

"Sorry he wouldn't let you search his place. Can't you get a warrant or something?"

"You misunderstood. He let me look around all I wanted. The upstairs closet was clean."

"That's not possible," I said angrily. "I'm telling you, it was *covered* with pictures of Ellen."

"Well, they're gone now. He must have realized what you two were after, so he got rid of the evidence."

"Hang on," I said. "I took some pictures. Let me send them to you, and then call me back, okay?"

"Fine. I'll be waiting for them."

After we hung up, I opened my phone, checked the camera, and pulled up the two shots I'd taken. It had been minimal light in there, and one of the shots hadn't turned out at all, but at least one of them showed a highlighted portion of the collage. I sent it to the sheriff, and then I waited for his return call.

I didn't have long to wait.

"There's no way that I can tell where that photograph was taken," he said with no preamble at all.

"I took it in Mitchell's upstairs closet. That has to count

for something."

"We'll look at him harder than we have been," Sheriff Croft said, "but as evidence, it's less than worthless."

"Even with my testimony about where I found it?" I asked.

"It's too soon to be talking about you testifying," he said. "We have to get a lot more on the man than that."

"You're going to at least try, though, aren't you?"

"We'll do what we can, but I can't promise you miracles, and you should know better than to ask for them. You know how this business works, Victoria."

I was disappointed with the results, but he was right. There was nothing I could about it at the moment. "Thanks for trying," I said.

"You're welcome. Listen, maybe I'll go back and lean on him a little harder this time."

"That would be great," I said.

"Oh, while I have you on the phone, it turns out that Crazy Betty watched Ellen and Wayne the entire time that they were picnicking. She said that they made such a cute couple that she couldn't stop watching them. Tell Ellen that as far as I'm concerned, she's in the clear, and if you see Wayne before I do, you can tell him, too."

"Thank you. They'll both be relieved," I said. "What happens now?"

"What do you think? We keep digging," the sheriff said, and then he hung up.

He wasn't the only one with a shovel, though.

Moose and I were going to continue to dig as well.

Maybe *somebody* would find a way to figure out how to prove that Mitchell had been the one to eliminate the competition for Ellen's affection, both past and present.

That's when it hit me. If Mitchell had indeed gotten rid of Gordon for his past sins, wouldn't Wayne be the next logical victim?

I called his shop, but he wasn't there.

I didn't have time to tell anyone where I was going. I had

to warn our friend before Mitchell decided to take everyone else who mattered out of Ellen's life.

Moose was still embellishing his story, clearly enjoying every moment of it, so I left him in the diner while I ran out to find Wayne and warn him.

As I was driving to the shop, my phone rang.

It was the sheriff. "I just wanted you to know that Mitchell was gone when I came back over here to talk to him again."

"That's not all that odd, is it?" I asked. "He's probably around somewhere."

"That's the thing. The door was unlocked and standing ajar, just like you said it was, so I checked it out. All of his personal stuff is gone. It couldn't have filled more than a suitcase in the first place, but there's nothing of his left at the house."

I felt my gut twist thinking that the killer might have gotten away when we'd been so close to nabbing him. "What are you going to do?"

"Don't worry. We'll find him. *This* is something the police are built for."

"I just hope that you catch him before anyone else gets hurt."

"We'll do our best," he said.

So then, Mitchell was on the run. Did that make him guilty, or just paranoid? Then again, why couldn't it be both? Either way, I hoped that the man turned up again soon.

"Is Wayne here?" I asked one of his mechanics as I hurried into the repair shop.

"No, he's out getting a part for me," the man said. "He'll be back in ten minutes, though, if you want to stick around."

"No, that's alright. Do you happen to know the name of the supply place where he went?"

"It's nothing as fancy as all that," he said. "He's just picking up a hose from the hardware store. Jack keeps a few things in stock that we need from time to time."

"I'll go there, then. Thanks."

As I drove to the hardware store, I had to park on the other side of the alley where Gordon was murdered. There were no spots in front of the hardware store, so I parked near A Close Knit World. There was a lovely display of yarn in the front window, and I considered the possibility of learning how to do it myself as I got out of my car. It might be something fun to do to unwind while Greg and I watched television at night.

I was in luck.

Wayne came out of the hardware store with a long thick hose in one hand.

"There you are. I've been looking for you," I said.

"What's going on? Did you catch the killer?"

"Maybe. I've got a hunch that we're getting close. That's what I need to discuss with you. Wayne, your life could be in danger."

"Why would anybody want to hurt me?" He looked startled by the very idea that he might be in danger.

"We think Mitchell Cobb might be knocking off rivals for Ellen's affection. If we're right, that puts you right in his crosshairs next."

Wayne shook his head. "Mitchell? You're not serious, are you?"

"Do I look like I'm kidding?"

"I've known Mitchell Cobb for years," Wayne said. "He doesn't seem the type."

"There's a lot that you don't know about him. Watch your back, and if he comes within a hundred yards of you, call the police."

"I'm not afraid of Mitchell Cobb," Wayne said.

"Well, maybe it's time that you were. Take this very seriously, Wayne."

"Okay, I get it. I'll be careful. Do the police know that he's a threat?"

"They're looking for him right now," I said. "On a happier note, Crazy Betty confirmed your alibi. She saw you with Ellen having your picnic in the park. As a matter of fact, she thought you two looked as though you belonged together."

"Maybe she can persuade Ellen of that," Wayne said a little wistfully.

"You two didn't break up, did you?"

"No, but she's doing her best to put on the brakes. We're not kids anymore, neither one of us, and I thought we were finally making some real progress, but with Gordon's murder, she's not even sure that she wants to *be* in another relationship just now."

I patted his arm. "Be patient, Wayne. Our girl's worth it."

"You're not telling me anything that I don't already know," he said. "It's just tough."

"Remember, anything worth having is worth fighting for," I said.

"That sounds more like Moose than you," the mechanic said with a slight smile.

"He might have said it first, but that doesn't make it any less true."

Wayne nodded, and then he shook the hose in the air. "I'd better get this back to Rupe. He's got a rush job that needs it."

"Just be careful," I reminded him once more. I was afraid that Wayne wasn't taking the threat seriously enough, but I wasn't sure what else I could do about it.

"Like I said, I've got it, Victoria."

I watched him get into his truck and drive away, and I wondered what I should do next. When in doubt, my fallback position was to always go to The Charming Moose, so that's where I headed.

Chapter 19

"Victoria, why did you take off like that without telling me where you were going?" Moose asked as I walked back inside the diner. "I looked away for a split second, and you were gone."

"Take it easy, Moose. I didn't do anything dangerous. I just needed to find Wayne to warn him about Mitchell."

"That was smart," my grandfather said. "If Mitchell is intent on knocking off rivals, then Wayne's in danger."

"That's exactly what I told him," I said.

"You still should have told me what you were up to," my grandfather said worriedly. It occurred to me that he was more concerned for my safety than the fact that I might have been investigating without him.

I kissed his cheek. "I'm okay."

"Fine. That's just fine." Moose paused, and then he asked, "So, where does that leave us?"

I looked around. "Is Ellen still here?"

"No, she went home with Opal and Robert. Why, do you need her?"

"I just wanted to share a little good news," I said. "With Crazy Betty confirming her alibi, she's off the hook with the sheriff. Wayne, too, as a matter of fact."

"Call her, then," Moose said.

"I don't think so. I have to give out a fair amount of bad news in my life, so I want to deliver something good like this in person."

"Then let's go. We can brainstorm about ideas about where Mitchell might be hiding while we drive over there."

I looked around the diner and saw that it was currently in Martha's and Jenny's most capable hands. "Why not? It sounds like a good plan to me."

"I have a question," I said to Moose as we drove toward Opal Hightower's house. "It might sound stupid, but there's something that's been bothering me."

"Let's hear it," Moose said. We often discussed new ideas when we were working on a murder case, and every street and avenue that we could come up with was always explored, no matter how crazy it might sound to the other at first.

"What if Mitchell is innocent?"

"From the description of that closet you found, I could hardly call him that," Moose said.

"I'm not pretending that he's not obsessed with Ellen to the point of sickness, but that doesn't make him a killer, no matter how convenient it appears to be at first glance."

"If it's not Mitchell, then who should we be looking at instead?" Moose asked.

"Well, our suspect list is nearly depleted. The only other names we have left are Opal and Robert. Could it be that we don't see the truth because we both want the killer *not* to be one of Ellen's parents?"

"Or both of them, for that matter," Moose said.

"Do you think they could have done it together?"

Moose appeared to think about it, and after thirty seconds, he said, "It's a possibility. What if Opal distracted Gordon while Robert snuck up behind him with a pipe?"

"I suppose that it's possible," I said. "Would it explain the bruises on Robert's hand?"

"He has bruises? When did this happen?"

"I didn't tell you about that? Sorry, that's all my fault. I was talking to him while I was waiting for you to pick me up, and I noticed that he was having a little trouble with his hand. He claimed that he hit a cinderblock wall in frustration, and I had no cause to doubt him at the time."

"What if he swung that pipe so hard that his knuckles connected with the wall near the hardware store as he made contact with Gordon's head? That could account for it as well."

"It makes me sick just thinking about Ellen's parents

ambushing the man like that."

"Remember, they were trying to protect her," Moose said.

"By killing the threat? You know what we have to do if this is true, Moose. We are going to *have* to tell the sheriff."

"I know that. But how are we going to find out for sure?"

"If they were working together, we need to split them up. When we get there, if we get the chance, I want to talk to Robert, and you can speak with Opal."

"Why can't I talk to Robert?" I asked.

"Victoria, we have to keep them apart. Let me do this my way. Please."

"Okay, but I don't like it. What if Robert decides to come after you?"

Moose shrugged. "Then I'll take care of him myself."

"I'm not sure this is the best idea, Moose. Why don't we tell Ellen the good news about her alibi, and then we can go straight to the sheriff with our alternate theory? He's a lot better equipped to handle something like this than we are."

"I hate to stop digging just when I feel as though we're closing in," he said.

"I know, but sometimes that's what we have to do."

When we got to Opal's, there was a problem, though. She was alone, working on a new knitting project as she answered the door.

"Is Ellen here?" I asked.

"She took the kids out for ice cream," Opal said. "Why? What's going on?"

"I just need to talk to her in person," I said.

"Well, you're welcome to wait here," Opal offered. "She shouldn't be that long."

"That's fine," I said. "I'll do that."

Moose asked offhandedly, "Do you know if Robert's home, by any chance?"

"He just went across the street. Why?" Opal asked him.

"I think I'll go talk to him for a minute," Moose said. He looked at me and asked, "Do you mind, Victoria?"

"Go on. It's fine with me," I said, though I wasn't entirely pleased with Moose's decision to press on without the sheriff's consent. "Remember, I'll be right here if you need me."

After my grandfather walked across the street, I kept watch on Robert's house, looking for any sign that Moose might be in trouble.

Opal must have noticed my constant vigilance. "You're not really waiting for Ellen, are you, Victoria?" she asked.

"I admit that it's not the only reason I'm watching outside," I said. I glanced back at her and saw that she was knitting furiously as we spoke, her hands moving with eerie, mechanical precision.

And that's when I got it.

One of the Hightowers had indeed killed Gordon Murphy, but I had a hunch that Robert hadn't had anything to do with it. Gordon had been killed between the hardware store and a shop that I knew Opal visited often, A Close Knit World. She must have spotted Gordon out the window as he walked past, and seizing the moment to protect her grandchildren, Opal had grabbed a pipe and ended his life.

"So, you know after all," she said the second she saw my face. "Are the police on their way?"

"I don't know what you're talking about," I said, trying my best to feign ignorance. She'd already killed once to protect her family. What was one more homicide?

"Don't lie to me, Victoria. You know that I did it. What gave me away?"

This was going nowhere. Maybe if I stalled her long enough, Moose would come back, and then it would be two against one. "Mostly it was the proximity of the crime scene to the yarn shop. You saw an opportunity to right a wrong, and you took it, didn't you? Robert doesn't know, does he?"

"I think he suspects something, but Ellen doesn't have a clue. So, what happens next?"

"If you turn yourself in, I'll do my best to see that it goes easier on you," I said.

"I can't do that, Victoria, and you know it."

"When you confessed to killing Gordon to me before, why didn't you admit to using the pipe on him?"

"I wasn't thinking straight," she said. "You pressed me, and I panicked."

"And I discounted your confession completely."

Opal nodded. "I realized that confessing wouldn't do Ellen any good, so when you dismissed it, I decided to take advantage of my second chance."

"You must have killed him close to two o'clock, because you sent your husband to pick up your grandchildren. That was out of the ordinary for you, wasn't it?"

"As much as Robert loves those two, nobody loves them more than I do. I couldn't stand the thought of losing them." She frowned, and then Opal added, "And I won't lose them now."

Uh oh. It appeared that we were going to have a problem here. "You have to give yourself up, Opal. It's the only way," I said.

Opal slipped the scarf she was knitting off the needles with great deliberation, and held one in each hand. Those things made nasty weapons when they were pointing straight at me. "I can think of another," she said as she started to move forward.

I felt my heart tighten. I didn't want to fight her, but in another second, I wasn't going to have any choice. I had to think fast and come up with a way to stop her.

Instead of looking for another weapon, though, I decided to use the one thing against her that had gotten her into trouble in the first place: her heart. "Opal, what happens if you do manage to get rid of me? I'm going to fight for my life, so things are going to get ugly here, but let's say that you succeed in killing me. Do you really want your daughter and your grandkids to walk through that door and find my body? There's going to be blood all over the place; I can guarantee you that."

"Of course. You're right," she said as the needles slipped through her fingers to the floor below. "What was I thinking?" At that instant, Opal started softly sobbing, and I knew it was crazy the moment I took that first step forward, but the woman was in pain. I hugged her, and the tears rushed out of her. "I'm so sorry," she kept repeating. I waited until her crying lessened, and then I took out my cell phone and called the sheriff. While we were waiting for him to show up, Moose and Robert came over together. I didn't need to explain a thing to them, because the second Opal saw Robert, she cried out, "I just wanted to save her, Robert. Will she ever forgive me?"

"Ellen loves you, Opal. She'll find a way."

Opal fell into his arms then, and she was still there when the sheriff showed up three minutes later to take her away to jail.

"I still can't believe that Ellen's mother killed Gordon," Greg said once Moose and I were back at the diner. Ellen had heard the news, and she was at the jail now, along with her kids and her father. The family was holding a vigil for Opal, and I was proud of my friend for standing by her mother in her time of need. None of us believed that the murder Opal had committed was okay, but everyone who had ever met Gordon Murphy could understand how the end of the bad egg came to be.

I was still discussing what had happened with Moose, Martha, and Greg when my cellphone rang. It was Rebecca Davis, and I'd been hoping that she'd call. "How's Opal holding up?"

"Surprisingly well," Rebecca said. "She gave me more details about what happened, so we have something to work with. I can't go into specifics, but apparently Gordon threatened her when she tried to convince him to leave Ellen and the kids alone. She says that he tried to attack her, and that she swung that pipe in self-defense."

"I thought he got hit from behind," I said.

"I asked her about that, and she said something distracted Gordon for a split second. When he turned his head to see if anyone was watching them, she hit him to keep him from killing her."

"Do you think that she's telling the truth?" I asked. I supposed that it *could* have been nothing but the facts, but it was all awfully convenient for Opal, and there was no one to refute her story, now that the other party in the conflict was dead.

"I don't know, but I do know one thing; I can sell it to a jury."

"Rebecca, aren't you at all concerned that she might just get away with cold-blooded murder?" I asked. I didn't know how my best friend could spend her days defending guilty people, putting them back on the streets, when they needed to be locked up behind bars.

"Who's to say *what* really happened? Opal's entitled to the best defense she can present, and I aim to do just that. Ultimately, her fate isn't in my hands, so I don't spend too many sleepless nights. Even if she does get off, I don't see her killing anyone else, do you?"

"No, if I had to guess, I'd say this was a one-time crime."

"There you go, then. Let's face it. There aren't *any* winners in this one, Victoria. Some days are like that, though. The best we can hope for is that no one innocent goes to jail. Speaking of folks who are innocent, the sheriff said they caught up with Mitchell Cobb. Turns out he decided to leave town because he was embarrassed that you saw his little shrine to Ellen."

"Why don't I feel good about any part of this case?" I asked.

"Do what I do. Try to find the silver lining," Rebecca said. "Ellen gets to keep her kids. That's a win in my book."

"No matter what the reason might be?" I asked.

"If it helps me get through the day, I'll take it," she said.

I caught everyone up with what happened, and there was a subdued feeling in the room after I was finished. Moose summed things up as he held us all close in his embrace. "We all need to take this as a sign that we should celebrate our family every chance we get. For all its flaws, we love each other, and in the end, that's what matters the most."

As we had a group hug, I had to wonder if Opal hadn't felt the same way. In a very real way, she'd sacrificed her own future for her grandchildren's, and I had to wonder if either one of my grandparents would have acted any differently than Opal if the roles had been reversed.

I quickly dismissed that thought, though.

I couldn't stand thinking about what Ellen and her family were going through, but I was thankful that it wasn't our clan experiencing it, whether that was a selfish way to think about things or not. Most of the people I loved were there in that room at that moment, and I was glad that each and every one of them were in my life. I knew that Ellen was going to face a difficult time ahead, but we'd all stand by her and see her through, no matter what.

After all, that was what family did, and while Ellen might not have shared any of our blood, she was just as much a part of The Charming Moose as any of us.

And in the end, that was what family was truly about, the love in our hearts, and not the blood that coursed through our veins.

GREG'S LASAGNA

My family truly enjoys this lasagna recipe. I'd love to be able
to tell you that it's been handed down from generation to
generation, but in fact, I saw this made on television one day
and then started tinkering with the recipe until I was happy
with it myself. I make a separate batch excluding all meat for
the vegetarian in my family, and it's equally good.

Ingredients

Olive oil, enough to coat the bottom of the pan
1 medium onion, chopped (about 1 cup)

Meat Options
Ground sausage, sweet or spicy
Ground beef
Or both
Or neither

Tomato sauce, 15 oz.
Salt, pepper to taste

Lasagna noodles, 8 oz.
Ricotta cheese, 15 oz.
Parmesan cheese, 1 cup
Mozzarella cheese, 16 oz.
1 egg, lightly beaten

Directions

Cover the bottom of a medium skillet with olive oil, then heat
to medium and add the chopped onion. After five minutes,
add the meat or meats of your choice and cook thoroughly.
After that is cooked, drain the meat/onion mixture, and then
add tomato sauce, salt and pepper. Simmer for twenty
minutes.
While this is simmering, cook the lasagna noodles, drain and

cool.

Next, mix the ricotta and Parmesan cheeses together, along with the beaten egg.

Now it's time to combine the ingredients. In a large rectangular pan (9 × 12 or 12 × 12), spoon out one third of the sauce on the bottom of the pan, then layer half the pasta, mozzarella, and ricotta mix. Add another third of the sauce, and then add more pasta, the cheeses, and then the rest of the sauce. Sprinkle the top with Parmesan cheese.

Bake this at 400° F for thirty to forty minutes.

Feeds 4 to 6.

MOM'S PANCAKES

We've been making this recipe for years, and it's a longtime family favorite. Weekends and pancakes seem to go together beautifully when we've all got a little more time to enjoy each other's company. We always heat our syrup on the stovetop, and we also add cooked spiced apples to the mix as well. Use real butter on these pancakes. It's worth the indulgence.

Ingredients

All-purpose flour, ¾ cup
Sugar, 1 tablespoon
Baking powder, 1 teaspoon
Salt, a dash
Whole or 2% milk, ½ cup
Egg, 1 whole, lightly beaten
Butter, 2 tablespoons, melted

Directions

Preheat the griddle or pan, greasing the bottom lightly with butter or cooking spray. In a medium bowl, sift together the flour, sugar, baking powder, and salt. In another bowl, add the milk, beaten egg, and melted butter and stir well.
Pour the liquid into the dry ingredients. Caution: stir the mixture only long enough until the dry ingredients are moist. Overstirring can ruin your pancakes.
Pour the batter onto the grill or into the frying pan, using about one quarter cup of batter. Cook until bubbles form on the top surface and the edges firm up, then turn the pancakes once.

Makes 4 to 5 large pancakes.

CPSIA information can be obtained at www.ICGtesting.com
Printed in the USA
LVOW13s2052070913

351440LV00001B/76/P